Any Given Moment

T.I. LOWE

DEDICATION

In memory of Benji Blanton

Football #82 and Baseball #31

And to his lovely mother, Mrs. Gail Blanton, who passed away while I completed this book. Mrs. Gail read the book and gave it her approval only weeks before she fell ill.

Love ya, my Gal Pal.

ACKNOWLEDGMENTS

Always a big thank you is needed for my readers. Without your enthusiastic cheering, I may not continue to be brave enough. You make me brave.

My Lowe and Stevens Bunch for putting up with my daydreaming. Love you all.

My beta readers—Sally Anderson, Kim Byrd, Trina Cooke, Christina Coryell, T Moise, and Jennifer Strickland. Thanks for having this ole girl's back. Your input and support are beyond appreciated.

Thanks to Albro Lee for inspiring Delilah with his unique truck creation.

My heavenly Father, you get all the credit for these stories. Thank you for allowing me to share you and your incredible love through these stories.

Chapter One

Some girls need a fruity drink with a colorful umbrella and tropical blue waves to find their happy place. Not me. All it takes is an icy-cold thermos of orange Gatorade and a sea of dewy green to help me find serenity. There's nothing like the sweet perfume of grass and earthiness first thing in the morning. Inhaling a deep breath of it, I lift my head to the sun and greet it with a smile. That warm beacon is just as anxious as I am to start this summer day.

Standing proudly off the ten yard line, I scan the patiently waiting rows of stadium seats—a fortress of black and gold that protectively overlooks the 120 yards of pristine turf. It's going to be a great season for the Texas Bobcats. No doubt about it.

Careful not to disturb the damp gems twinkling along the surface of the football field, I make my way over to my mower. The mean-green machine sits stoically at the back bay, reels sharpened and ready for action. It's time to get my dutiful day as this fine stadium's head groundskeeper underway. Before I climb on the mower, the echoing sound of a door banging shut from the home locker room tunnel grabs my attention. Taking pause, I'm a little surprised to find none other than Wiley Black. This ridiculously talented quarterback caused the football nation to mourn when his professional career ended in just its first glorious season. It was a flawless season that was only one infamous game away from the game of all games. A season football history won't forget any decade soon.

Shaking off my own bitter disappointment for that terrible fate, I regard his large, lean form as he lugs giant buckets and a mesh bag full of footballs along with him. Hermes is what the sports world nicknamed him way back in his days of college football. GQ looks and a rare talent, he definitely is the modern day Greek god of athleticism.

Cringing, I helplessly watch on as he wrecks my perfectly dewy field by walking right on it like he owns the place. I'm near the back bay, and he takes no time to check for spectators. Wiley has already ruined my plans for mowing, so I scoot a bit deeper out of sight to observe him.

Wiley dumps the bag at the fifty and moves to the end zone with determination. He has a smooth stride that gives away no evidence as to the damage hiding underneath the leg of his black track pants. The only thing it gives away is the certitude of whatever he's about to do. My curiosity is piqued as I watch him set up three barrel-sized buckets in front of the goal—left edge, center, and right. Turning on his heel, Wiley beelines it back to the fifty, hat shoved low on his head and shrouding his angular features. After a quick glance at his watch, he pulls the first of probably forty or so footballs out of the bag.

My heart picks up its pace with anticipation of seeing this legend in action. It's definitely a gift I wasn't expecting to stumble upon this fine July morning. He adjusts his position a few steps before launching the pigskin in a perfect spiral. The ball ricochets off the left upright in a gratifying ping before descending to the barrel. When the ball bounces off the rim and lands in the wet grass, neither one of us seems too thrilled by it. I'm gonna have no dew left to guide my mower if he keeps this up. I don't need it, but I do find satisfaction with it directing my path.

With no noise passing inside the brick and steel walls of the stadium, his deep sigh easily reaches my ears from where I'm hiding behind him. Wiley pulls off his hat and runs his hand through his dark, wavy hair in frustration.

The fangirl in me wants to rush the field and beg for his autograph like some psycho. Behaving myself instead, I stay rooted in my spot and take in his every move like he's some abstract artwork needing to be studied. Thoroughly.

After cramming the hat back on, he swipes another ball and readjusts his feet once more. Launching from a slightly new alignment, the ball collides with the upright once again, but this time it makes it into the barrel with precision. Hermes hasn't lost his touch.

This drill continues with consecutive *pings* ringing out until each barrel has its own share of balls and my grass only shares company with that very first ball. Each throw is precise with its path in such a severe focus I want to throw my hands in the air and scream, "Why him?"

Wiley Black disappears back into the tunnel as quietly as he appeared—his meeting with his new home, Cooper Stadium, complete. My day finally gets underway at seven, one hour later than my normal morning schedule. Great. Now the entire day will be off kilter. Mounting the mower, I set out to make up some time.

I'm a rare oddity in my *field* of work—some pun intended. Women are not easily found in my position. I'm responsible for this massive ninety-seven thousand square foot stadium that can hold seventy-seven thousand fans on any given game day. I take pride in the work I've done here for the past six years, but the controls have only been placed in my hands for two.

I literally pulled my time in flowerbeds for the first part of my career with my male chauvinistic pig for a boss thinking that was all my girlie-self could handle. It was one sweet day at his retirement party when I was named his replacement. So I've earned the right to forbid a soul on this field until I get the privilege of mowing it. Hermes better be glad I'm a fan.

Cramming in my earbuds and cranking up Skillet to full eardrum-bursting volume, I direct the machine to get on with it.

*****

The day scoots by with field prep and tending to the tall order of new flowers that are set to arrive in the morning. I'm still a sucker for the bed designs, but I have a head horticulturist who handles the hefty job nowadays. All I have to do is sign my signature of approval and try to keep out of Benji's way, which is easier said than done.

Benji is a big teddy bear, and a man who knows how to get things done. I'll never forget the first week I worked with him. We have what we call the flower truck. It's just an old beat-up pickup that we putter around in with all of our planting supplies. Texas heat is harsh and that truck has no air conditioner. Benji had enough of it one day, so while I headed in for our lunch break, he chose to work on the truck. I came back out an hour later and found Benji sitting in the truck minus doors.

I asked him, "Benji, didn't this truck have doors before lunch?"

"Yep. Now it has air conditioning."

And that was that. The doors are long gone, but the truck still putts around with great ventilation. I can't help but smile just thinking about it.

Today is special, so I treat my crew by having Renata's Cantina delivered. Being neighbors with Mexico may have drawbacks, but I like to focus on the perks. You can't get authentic tamales or enchiladas just anywhere.

As I'm cramming my fourth tamale in my mouth, my head irrigation tech, Buck, pushes into my shoulder. "Dang, Sam. You eat like a hog." Laughter rings out.

Looking around the long table at the crew members all donning the required uniform of white T-shirt with the Bobcats Grounds Crew logo and black cargo pants, I send them all a glare. It's the uniform of my choice. Before I took over, we all had to wear stiff uniform pants with a button-up work shirt that was more fitting for a garage mechanic. It's too hot in these southern parts to not be comfortable.

"I work my butt off around this place. Literally." I pause to swallow the substantial bite of spicy goodness. "I need lots of fuel." Taking in the O of Buck's rounded gut, I grimace dramatically.

"What?" he mutters around a sloppy mouthful of enchilada.

"I'm obviously not working you hard enough, old man." I give his solid girth a playful pop, causing a bark of laughter from the crowd.

"What's with this treat today, Sam?" Trey, my assistant crew leader, asks.

I grab a fresh napkin and wipe my mouth before

answering, "Cooper just signed Wiley Black as head coach for the Bobcats."

The break room is muted instantly in absolute awe—food is being held frozen in mid-bite and faces slack with wonder. Oh yeah. Hermes is that legendary.

Leave it to my one and only non-football fan in the room to break the silence. "Who's that?" Zane asks, and is rewarded with every other member in the room throwing trash at him. He flings his hands up defensively and starts batting the napkins and wrappers back in their direction. "Chill."

"Black was considered the quarterback of the century until an injury ended all of our dreams for him." Trey shares this reverently and everyone minus Zane shudders at the memory.

The tamales begin to churn in my puny gut as flashes of bone and gore protruding through the skin of Wiley's lower right leg pass through my memory.

Zane still looks unperturbed until Colton, my other assistant, pulls up what I'm guessing is the image of Wiley's well photographed injury and shows it to him.

The guy's face pales before us. "Dude."

This is all he has to say. Zane is sort of out of place here, with no interest in the sport we all idolize. This hippie-looking guy, with his long blond hair and tanned skin, wandered into the stadium one day and has never left. I eventually put him on the payroll after discovering he has a spectacular knack for painting fields. He is a unique one with an artistic flair that follows him wherever he drifts, and I've grown right attached to him.

Scanning this crowd, I could say the same for each one of my crew members. We make a pretty good team.

"All right, ladies, lunchtime is over." I push away from the table and commence to handing out afternoon assignments. There's a lot to do before training day arrives in only one week.

The remaining work hours race by and it's three before I know it. That's one of the perks of this job—early start to the day equals early dismissal. The crew is gone, but my day only ends after a walkthrough. Leaving the intense sun out by the entrance, I'm peacefully enveloped by the cool dimness of the tunnel that leads to the home locker room. I've seen no more sign of Hermes, but I head through to be sure he's made his way out before locking up.

The gold tunnel has the Bobcats black and white emblem blazing along the wall to my right. It's some impressive artwork, but the tunnel instinctively beckons me to the left wall. My fingers reach out and dust along the words of Hebrews 12:1 as I pass by.

Therefore, since we are surrounded by such a great cloud of witnesses, let us throw off everything that hinders and the sin that so easily entangles, and let us run with perseverance the race marked out for us.

I repeat the verse as my fingers play over them. This is a ritual all players and coaches perform not just before each game, but any time they enter the field through this tunnel. The stadium owners never want the team to forget who granted them with the extravagant gift of being allowed to play professional football—God.

Repeating the verse once more, after I find the place as empty of life as a ghost town, I call it a day.

Chapter Two

Broad shoulders, a head full of dark hair that the breeze doesn't even dare mess with, and tanned taut muscles... There's no denying the view is stellar, but it's putting a considerable cramp in my style. Well, more like my schedule.

Wiley has been at it every morning for the past week, and I'm reaching my boiling point. He's thrown my entire routine off, and I'm also going to have to add repainting the goal posts to the to-do list soon if he keeps up his abuse of them. I've already voiced my concerns with Cooper, but all he offered in response was a toothy grin and has taken up a cushiony seat in his owner's box suite to watch the show ever since.

Whatever. Training camp kicks off tomorrow, and so the list for field prep is a mile long. The press will be allowed for the first hour, and I want nothing less than an impeccable stadium backdrop to represent the Texas Bobcats.

Standing in position, I shove on my Ray-Bans and readjust my wide-brimmed bucket hat, pushing a few black strands back under that have wiggled their way free. Checking my watch, I see I've given him thirty minutes with no plans on giving him another second. He walks off towards the buckets, so I take my opportunity to sprint out and gather his mess off my fifty yard line.

As I'm dumping the armful close to the tunnel, I hear the raspy timbre of his voice call out to me. "Hey! Hey you, kid!"

My body reacts as though a chill just skated across it, but I ignore it, as well as Wiley, and keep booking it towards my mower.

I'm about to shove my earbuds in to drown him out, when a heavy hand lands on my shoulder and then commences to turning me forcefully in his direction. This guy is definitely used to having his authority respected. I keep my social standings intact and allow him to be boss.

He seeks out the photo ID dangling around my neck. "Sam, look man..." Wiley stumbles over his last word, so I'm guessing my boobs have just registered as his confused gaze stops in that vicinity. "You're a girl."

I know I shouldn't bring any more attention to this certain area, but my sarcasm overrules my better judgement. Gasping, I pat my chest dramatically. "Dang it! I think you might be right!"

A few beats tick by before he snaps out of his shock, and a look of annoyance registers along his handsome features.

"Look, kid. Smart-mouthing me isn't wise." He's towering at least a foot above me in a threatening stance, but he doesn't know I'm not the type to be intimidated so easily.

I could go two ways with this—show the man some respect or sass him some more. Sass is calling out to me in a high-pitched whine, but I tell her to hush up. No need in getting into trouble with the head coach this early on. Instead of giving him what he deserves, I pull out my manners like the good ole southern gal my momma and daddy raised me to be—not an easy task for this here tomboy to keep on point.

"Yes, sir. Sorry."

"Why'd you move my stuff?" He motions towards his pile of belongings.

"I've got to get this field mowed and prepped. You're putting me behind schedule."

Now that giant hand gestures towards me. "You?" Looking around the stadium in disbelief, he continues, "*You* have to mow all of this by your scrawny self?"

Well now, that just doesn't go over too well with me. At. All. I hold steady with not giving him any more lip, but my stubborn hands find their way to my hips.

"Yes, sir. Been doing it for the past two years." I release a hand and wave towards the vibrant sea of lush, green turf. "And I haven't killed it yet."

Yes, I know that last part might be interpreted as

giving lip, but it slipped out without my permission.

With a skeptically raised eyebrow, he says, "Well, I'll let you get to it. Sorry I got in your way, kid."

Wiley abandons our confrontation and goes to gather his stuff before my lips conjure anything polite to say. I think some more as I watch on. Nope. Still can't think of anything. Looking down, I guess my baggy clothes can be a bit concealing with the fact I'm nowhere near being a kid. I'm actually knocking on thirty's door.

Shrugging my frustration off, I set out to do my job so the arrogant pig can do his.

*****

Five o'clock arrives early this morning with lots of anticipation crackling through the air. Today, I get to see the goods along with the army of press, and my stomach won't stop squeezing in eagerness. I'm glad to have the field to myself for the first time in forever. With the stadium lights up, I'm able to mow as easily as in the middle of the day. The rest of the crew is scurrying around watering the freshly planted flowerbeds. And those babies are spectacular. All of the beds are blanketed in a thick array of black, gold, and white perennials, but the pièce de résistance is the main entrance bed that rests on the grand hill where fans pass before they reach the gates. Benji drew the outline of the bobcat with Viola 'Black Magic' and then filled it in with Basket of Gold. White perennials box the entire piece in and boy does it make a statement. Benji is a planting genius. I'm hoping to have a photographer out here later in the week to capture it for promos. The guy's name is JP Thorton and he comes highly recommended. I've seen some of his work, so I know he'll see the stadium properly.

At seven sharp, the gates open and a caravan of shiny cars—hot off the high-dollar dealership lots—file into the team parking lot. I've picked a spot inside on the second floor to watch the show.

In the midst of blinged-out sports cars and souped-up trucks sits my rusty 1954 Chevy pickup. The only paint existing on the truck is on the hubcaps, which are a bright blue. My favorite characteristic is by far the exterior cargo light. It is an actual porch light fixture with a hand-pull. The back side rails are pretty unique as well. It looks like someone just chopped down four thin trees, stripped them of their bark, and mounted two on each side. It's awesome and definitely one of a kind.

Each polished vehicle gives my Delilah plenty of room. Not a soul parks beside her or in front. It's quite comical to see these real-life giants try climbing out of those tight cars. Laughing privately, I head back outside to the main entrance and watch on as media vans take up their spots in guest parking. My skin prickles with expectancy for the new season.

I know this stadium like the back of my hand—I'm privy in knowing all of the shortcuts and some secret tunnels—so I maneuver to the field before the first cameraman has time to set up his tripod. No grounds crew member is allowed in here today, but me. I take my spot near the back bay and prepare to take in what can only be described as a well-orchestrated circus. This morning is strictly for show and not even ten minutes pass before it gets underway with whistles blowing and cameras clicking.

My eyes betray me as they seek out Wiley Black. The man's presence is demanding, so I can't help myself. He is properly dressed for the cameras—in khaki pants and a gold-colored polo with the Bobcats logo neatly stitched on the shirt. The other coaches match his attire, but somehow don't compare. Even so, everyone looks polished and photo ready. All the Bobcat giants stand at attention in their gold T-shirts and black shorts, fresh and eager.

My crew set up obstacle courses and drill sets this morning, and I watch now as the players descend to their designated posts. This stuff makes good photo and video ops, but that's about it. As the team puts on a show, my focus goes back to Black, who is observing it all by the sideline as reporter after reporter gets their five minutes with him. Sometime during this hoopla, he looks my way and actually gives me a head nod in acknowledgement.

Well. Don't I feel special now?

This part of the business bores me, so I leave them and get on with my day. I'm more anxious to get to see the *real* practices.

Chapter Three

Wiley Black goes from taking over *my* field to now kicking me off it altogether during practices, except for emergencies. I guess that head nod the other day wasn't a gesture of welcome, but a warning. Don't ask how much that ticks me off. *Jerk.*

A leaking sprinkler head has granted me a pass for the day. I bring Trey for backup since Buck is hip deep in a hole near section C of the parking lot. We have a picnic area over there and a main valve isn't playing pretty.

The needed tools for the leaky job are obvious, but I decide to leave them behind in order to buy me some more time on the field. Trey has already called me out on it, but after explaining to him we are about to perform some major dilly-dallying he's game.

Before walking onto the field, we both pull on our shades. The guy even has a black bucket hat exactly like mine. A chuckle slips out as I look him over.

"What?" Trey mutters, sounding distracted.

Motioning between us, I snicker. "Twins."

"Nah-ah. I'm a good three inches taller than you."

17

I scoff. "Please. You're not that much taller. But you are older." By only a month, but it still counts.

We bicker about this until we reach the sprinkler head. Luck would have it, the leak is right by the sideline benches where everyone is congregated. Coach Jerk seems to have just wrapped up a pep talk and is ordering the first string to the line of scrimmage. I angle myself just so, with hopes of catching a few plays while I fix the minor problem.

"You gonna be long, kid?" That gruff voice sounds against my back, riling me up.

"I have a name. It's Sam or Shaw. And if you want me to acknowledge you from now on, I suggest you pick one." I keep my voice low so none of his players hear me sassing him. Trey is crouched down in front of me, so I can see his eyes bugging out in disbelief from behind his shades.

I stay in my place and start unscrewing the busted head.

Wiley must have decided to just ignore the comment altogether and asks again, "How long?"

"Thirty minutes tops and I'll be off *your* field." I firmly clamp my lips shut after this slip. Seems I'm on a roll today. Trey wiggles uncomfortably as though he's gonna pee his pants. Wiley Black is nothing shy of intimidating.

Wiley says nothing else, but his shadow leers over me as I inspect the problem. I hear him sigh deeply in impatience, but it doesn't hurry me up in the slightest. I'm not in a compliant mood today.

18

"Trey, would you go grab a coupling, shovel, channel locks, tape, and some glue?"

"Sure, boss." I know he throws that last word in there for effect.

"And a new sprinkler head," I add as he hurries off. He recognizes the request with a hand wave over his shoulder.

I sit on my haunches and wait. As soon as Wiley's shadow leaves me alone, I text Trey to take his time. I want to see some field action. I catch one play and am not pleased by what I witness. The offensive line is sloppy. Another play goes down and the head quarterback Grant is not being covered well at all.

Glancing at Wiley, I notice him honed in on that line as well. He only lets it go for another play before he barks at them to clean it up. The snap of the ball and then the bodies crashing rings out and again the QB is tackled. I've had enough at this point and am ready to holler at them to wake up. Thank goodness, I hold it in and let the coach do his job.

Calling the entire team in, they gather around Wiley. All are red-faced, breathless, and sweating like pigs. I get it though. I'm only sitting on my backside in this Texas heat and have sweat trickling down my back. That's not an excuse for their sluggishness. Most of them get paid seven plus figures to be able to handle it.

Grant tosses Wiley the ball before the fuming coach sets out to serving the linemen a decent butt chewing. It's obvious they are the focus and all of the other players keep a slight distance from them. Not Grant. He shares the blame and stands stoically with his linemen.

"The ink isn't even dry on your contracts yet. Do you realize how replaceable you are? You're being paid to do a certain job and I've not seen you earn one cent on this field since you strutted your egos out here. So do your job or face the consequences." Wiley pauses the speech to pace in front of the group for a few beats. It's evident he is trying to tamp down his anger.

My phone pings a new message, but I'm too enthralled to check it. It's probably Trey and he can wait. The radio on my side will go off next if it's urgent.

Waving the ball in front of them, he continues, "I don't see an individual here. I see one unit with the sole purpose of moving this ball to the end zone. If a part of this unit doesn't perform correctly, something breaks and will need to be replaced." He has shorts on today and although he sports a very nice set of legs, the mean thick scar is on full display. I notice all eyes have dropped to it. "Get the ego-chip off your shoulder and do your job!" As he yells this, I follow his eyes over to Jones, whose stats declare he has football magic coursing through his veins. I guess all that magic comes with a hefty arrogance.

Wiley shouts for them to get back on the field and Mr. Magic saunters over to his position without a care in the world. I've studied the roster and have observed this inside-look enough over the years to call this one pretty clear—too young and too naïve to be allowed in, but too blame talented not to. Sadly, the team has to pay until these kinds of bigheaded punks grow up.

The other linemen are letting him take the attitude-lead, and I'm willing to bet all eight idiots are about to pay dearly for this poor choice.

Trey tosses the supplies beside the head, startling the mess out of me. "What did I miss?"

Grabbing the shovel, I start poking around the head distractedly. "Nothing, but I got a feeling it's about to get a lot more interesting." We both half-heartedly work on repairing the leaking adapter as we try to inconspicuously watch the show.

Sure enough, after one play, Wiley has reached his limit and calls the offensive linemen and Grant back. The other coaches take over the rest of the group and carry on.

"What's your job, Jones?"

Wiping his brow, Jones says, "Protect the quarterback's a—"

"No profanity on my field or you'll be forking out that fine stated in your contract. There are enough words in the English language, and I won't be having my team sounding like vulgar illiterates." Wiley is all but in this punk's face.

I expect a respectable *sorry sir*, but Jones only offers a grunt instead. *Idiot.* I tsk before I can stop myself, but no one acknowledges me.

"Sam," Trey warns quietly. I refocus on fitting the new coupling in place and leave the coach to do his job, but I can't help listening.

"The quarterback is your job. You get paid to protect him and the ball. Let your guard down and what happens?"

"He botches the play," Clark, a three-hundred-plus-pound guard, mutters.

Trey and I roll our eyes at the same time, as I hear a derisive huff escape Wiley. Shaking my head, I goof with the tape to look like I'm making progress as Trey fiddles with the adapter. Neither one of us is making a lick of headway.

"*He*?" Wiley asks this with enough coolness to send a chill through this ninety-eight-degree day. "*We* is the *only* term acceptable on this field. Something you should have learned way back on those high school fields you grew up on."

They all mumble out various yessir comments.

Shaking his head, Wiley passes the ball to Grant. "For the rest of this practice, your sole purpose is to carry the weight of your quarterback."

They all nod like they get it, but they're not even close.

"Jones, you'll start it off. Pick Grant up and start doing laps. When you can't carry him any longer, you pass him to another lineman. The rest of you follow along and be ready to help carry Grant."

Confusion mars each guy's face, but then that transforms into dreadful understanding.

"But, sir, that's two hours," the center comments.

"You're correct, Hoffman. And if so much as a shoe string from Grant's cleat touches the ground, the entire group of you, minus Grant, will be benched the first game of the season."

"But, sir—"

"Get on with it." Wiley points to Grant.

Jones swiftly picks up Grant's six-four frame and drapes him over his arm, before taking off along the sidelines with the rest shuffling behind them.

"What if I gotta take a leak, sir?" Grant calls out.

"Do what you have to do, but your foot best not touch one blade of grass or all your linemen pay the consequence."

They set out, so Trey and I refocus on our task, both fighting grins. Sensing Wiley shift his stance closer to me, I get a little nervous.

"Do you get paid to supervise my practices?" He doesn't call me kid, and I guess that should earn him a few points, but his harsh tone wipes them out.

I take his lead from earlier and completely ignore the question. I figure it's time to speed things up and get out of Dodge. Trey seems to be on the same page, because the weasel has already grabbed up the unneeded tools and has hightailed it on me. Talk about loyalty.

Standing up and brushing the muck off my pants, I say, "I'm done, Coach." Without waiting for a response, I follow in Trey's abandoning wake.

ANY GIVEN MOMENT

Chapter Four

The last two months have flown by in rapid speed with me keeping clear of Wiley while he's on my field. Doesn't mean I'm not supervising some of his practices from a conveniently unlocked box suite. It's my right to keep an eye on my field. We have a perfectly maintained practice field, but Wiley refuses to use it most of the time.

Standing in the packed stands, tingles zip up and down my spine as "Centuries" starts booming through the stadium's sound system. The acknowledging roar of the crowd is deafening, as an army of black and gold rushes the field.

A glorious sun is shining this fine September Sunday, and the field looks awesome from this angle. The only thing not perfect is the guy standing next to me. I've never seen him in my life, but he's carrying on like we're engaged. I've already shrugged his heavy arm off my shoulder one too many times in the past fifteen minutes. From the rancid smell of his breath and the noticeable sway, I'd say he started his celebrating yesterday. All I want is to watch this game, and my *drunken fiancé* is ruining it. He finally turns his attention to his buddy, so I scurry away. I've got roughly ten good minutes to find me another spot before kick-off. The only option is the box suites.

Pushing through the thick crowd with my mind made up, I hurry to my office upstairs. I can't blend in while wearing my uniform, so I strip out of it as soon as I lock my door. Pulling on a pair of black slacks and a creamy-gold top, I glance nervously at the clock as I yank a brush through my black mane. I shove my feet into a pair of too-high heels while working my hair into a loose bun. The mirror on the wall reflects the impatience in my light-blue eyes. Those babies are framed with a thick fringe of lashes so mascara isn't needed, but I do swipe some lip gloss on as I grab my box suite pass on the way out the door.

Today is a special game. It's opening day and Cooper Stadium has the honor of playing host, so I know the big guy will be in the main suite with the investors—great advantage for me with trying to sneak myself in. I'm getting right hungry, so I choose the VIP suite, since I know the menu for this room today includes baby back ribs and potato salad. The room is all abuzz and everyone is busy watching the field. The sweet, tangy aroma of barbeque sets my mouth to watering, but I leave the food alone for the time being and scoot over to claim a seat up front. Nope. I'm not shy.

"Hello, dear," a lovely voice greets from beside me.

I glance over with enough politeness before honing back to the field in time to see the kick-off. "Hello. Isn't this exciting?"

The older lady chuckles warmly. "It most certainly is—new coach and practically a new team."

"No doubt," I say, jumping to my feet when one of our guys goes down. Ugh. And the game just got started! We all clap when he gets up and walks off the field unassisted. Thank goodness.

"So you like this sport?"

"Absolutely," I answer as the opposing team in silver and dark-blue snaps the ball. One of our big boys stops it before they can make the first down. "Yeah!" I shout along with most of the room.

"What do you think about the new coach?" the dark-grey haired lady asks.

My lips twitch with wanting to release a grin when I meet her green eyes. "Your son is the best quarterback our country has ever had, and I'm putting my money on him being the best coach as well." I squeeze her shoulder when I notice a pink blush color her cheeks. "It's a pleasure to meet you, Mrs. Black. I'm Samantha Shaw. Now, no more fishing for compliments, young lady." You can tell she is a proud momma and she most certainly has the right to be.

My mock-scold causes her husband, Nolan Black, to bark out in laughter. He reaches around her from where he's sitting on her other side to shake my hand. He's a big man with a mostly bald head, but I see a lot of Wiley's handsome features were divvied out from him.

"The stadium is spectacular," he comments, and now I do grin.

"Oh yes. And those logos painted on the field are extraordinary," Mrs. Black chimes in.

"Why thank you, Mr. and Mrs. Black. I completely agree."

"Please call us Maggie and Nolan," she corrects.

"Does it matter which?" I ask as they laugh. I bring my attention to the spectacular logo they were bragging about and cringe. "Oh no."

"What's wrong, dear?"

"Nothing," I mutter to her as I text Zane to meet me in my office first thing in the morning. Sure enough, the logo is beyond awesome, but it's not the one I gave him to paint. Yes, the company name is there and all the info, but the design is nothing like the original.

After the second quarter begins, with only a three-point field goal being scored by the Bobcats, my phone pings with a new text. I'm expecting it to be Zane, but find Cooper's assistant letting us know that all department heads are to meet an hour after the game in his office. I don't consider myself a department head and he knows this, so I'm not surprised when the message comes through—*that includes you, Miss Shaw*. Great! I know it's the logo, too. That was a costly mistake.

Shoving the phone in my pocket along with my worries, I refocus on the field. Offense is at the line of scrimmage and my gut tenses. The ball doesn't get very far. Not good. "Come on Jones!" I holler like he can actually hear me.

"What's wrong with that big boy?" Maggie asks.

"Jones is having a hard time seeing past the stars swirling around his head to do his job. Fame does that to some of these boys." I blurt this out without much thought. Several sharp looks tell me I need to remember to think next time.

I settle back down in my chair and watch with frustration coursing through my veins. Another play and Grant goes down. "Pull him, Black!" I yell with my heart picking up speed. Maybe I should have watched from home…

My eyes scan the sideline until they land on Wiley, and watch on as he yanks the headset off while yelling with flailing arms towards Jones. I happily settle down when he takes to yelling in the player's face and then points behind him. A timeout is called. Wiley threads his hands through his hair and that movement has captured my rapt attention. I do appreciate how that gold polo shirt stretches tightly across those well-defined shoulders and how he fills a pair of black pants out nicely…

"Honey. Yoo-hoo." Maggie is saying something but I've not caught a word of it.

"I'm sorry. What was that?"

"It's only Wiley's first game. He'll get them straightened out." Momma Bear is taking up for her baby and I don't blame her.

I pat Maggie's arm and give her a reassuring smile. "I'm confident he will."

Halftime shows up before we know it, with me digging into the glorious grub. I notice a gathering of tall, underfed beauties staying as far away from the food as possible. It's as though they fear the calories may reach out and grab ahold of them if they get too close. Maggie is filling a plate beside me, and I just can't help myself.

Nodding towards the scantily clad Barbie Dolls, I ask, "Which one of those lovelies belongs to your son?"

"Oh. None, dear. My Wiley says he doesn't have time for such..." She trails off. I'm guessing he's still licking his wounds from his very public break-up. Not to mention the fact his ex-fiancée moved right on to the next up-and-coming football star, without so much as a glance back.

I don't bug her for any more dirt. It's none of my business anyway. I do take my overfilled plate of ribs and elbow myself in the midst of the starved beauties—just for meanness. They scatter like flies on the run from the flyswatter. A chuckle slips from me as I dig into the tangy barbeque goodness.

In the second half, it's very noticeable our players have settled down and are playing good enough to pull the win—28 to 24. I enjoyed my time with the Blacks and am relieved how the game turned out.

What I'm not relieved about is sitting in this office with about a dozen bigwigs. I'm back in my uniform and really need to get to work, but I'm stuck against my will, might I add. The meeting trickles on and I find my mind wandering along the long list of afternoon tasks until an elbow nudges me in the side. As the elbow retreats, I notice the room has gone silent. Great. *What did I miss?*

"Miss Shaw." The big guy in charge drawls this out. I instantly seek him out and find him perched grandly at his desk. Stark white hair—thick and impeccable—gives the scowl he's wearing a softness without meaning to.

"Yes, sir?"

"What do you have to say about the logo mishap?"

"I think the guy has too much talent to be wasting it on spray-painting fields." My gaze roams the group and discovers each suit with their own scowl. Tough crowd. "But it was very inappropriate. Zane will be given a week's suspension without pay." Which is perfect because next week's game is away.

The group goes a few rounds about the logo debacle until the meeting comes to an end. I try scooting my body in the midst of the crowd exiting in hopes of making a clean getaway.

"Miss Shaw."

Ugh. I should have made a run... no, a sprint for it. Too late.

"May I have a word with you, privately?" Cooper asks.

"Umm... I've got quite a busy schedule..." Catching the expression on his face, it's clear he's not asking. "Sure." Dragging my feet over to a chair in front of his desk, I plop down and wait for the rest of the room to finish clearing out.

Easing back into his leather throne, Cooper gets right to it. "Samantha, I can't have you costing us ten thousand dollars just because you want to make some kid your pet project."

"That's a ridiculous statement, Dad." I sit straighter in my chair to better defend the situation. "Zane was just testing the waters." A reddening is creeping along his neck, causing me to reword that with hands held up in justification. "A costly testing, I know. He won't ever do it again."

"Next stunt like that, he's to be terminated immediately, and you'll be forking out the fine from your own pocket."

"Wow, that's a little steep for a head groundskeeper's salary."

"Don't get smart with me, young lady."

Ouch. I felt the sting from his sternness all the way from here. I guess my dad is in no playing mood. "Yessir."

"You're part owner of this stadium and team. You know what's at stake."

"Yessir."

Dad sold me half the company the day I graduated college for a hefty ten bucks—that's what I had in my pocket and that's what he accepted. Yes, I'm blessed. No, I don't take it for granted.

"Enough of that. I want you in the owner's box next game." The red from his neck is gone now that he thinks he has the upper hand.

"No can do. I've got to be keeping a closer eye on field situations from now on." Crossing my arms, I wait for the red to creep back up, but am surprised when Dad chuckles.

"You're as stubborn as your—"

"Dad," I add quickly. And he knows it's the truth. I catch the ghost of a smile.

"Samantha, you've got to quit hiding in the shadows. You're almost thirty years old, and it's time you stop playing in the dirt."

Oh no. Here comes the settling down lecture. "Dad, I really have work to do. Please not today," I whine.

He brushes the topic away with a wave of his hand and moves on. "What do you think about Black?"

"He's taking his job very seriously. He won't be tolerating his players dropping the ball."

"Good."

"Although, I'm not crazy about him kicking me off my field. And he got ahold of me for watching his practice the other day. Said I didn't get paid to supervise him."

We both crack up at this, because I actually do get paid for just that. "Maybe it'll do you good to have someone around here who can handle putting you in your place."

"Dad!" He knows that's not fair.

Again, he brushes that topic off and rapidly moves to another. "Your presence is requested at the game day opening party tonight."

"Requested?" That's not technically an *order*.

"Encouraged."

"Encouraged?" That can be *discouraged*.

"Dang it, Sam. You're ordered to be there."

"Well, there's just no wiggle room with you, is there?" I scoff and cross my arms.

"No. And be sure to wash up beforehand. Your mother has a new dress and all that stuff ready for you at the house."

I glance at my watch and slowly shake my head. "I don't know if I'll have time to make it out to the *house*." I exaggerate house because the word just doesn't suit a multimillion-dollar mansion sitting grandly in the center of a four-hundred-acre ranch. You can get lost in it, and I'm glad dad had me a cottage built on the property a few years back.

"Samantha." That's all he has to say to let me know that there's no wiggle room here either.

"Yessir." I make a beeline for the door before he can request anything else. He and Mom wanted a son, but they got me. I'm a tomboy so it seems they would be happy to get a close second, but they're always on me to act more like a lady. Good grief.

*****

Running my fingers through my newly obtained glossy-black waves, which the stylist brushed into submission, I scoot through the doors of the owner's suite at the stadium eight minutes late. I try blending in the crowd and acting as though I've been here all along, but Dad is like the time police and has me in his sights in seconds.

He's in front of me just that fast, too, and is about to say something when I stop him.

"I know. I'm late. You should send me straight home for punishment," I mumble while accepting his quick hug.

"I was going to say you look beautiful." Dad steps back and gives me a pointed look, daring me to refute his declaration.

My palms smooth down the length of the fancy black gown. The texture is silky and cool to the touch. "Well, the team of stylists Mom had attack me gave it their best shot." I shrug.

Dad inspects my feet with a sigh of relief. "Thank goodness."

"What are you thanking goodness for now?"

"Your mother talked you into proper lady shoes, too."

I glance down in disgust at the four-inch gold stilettos. "There's nothing proper about these dang things." I lick my lips absently. Ugh. I'm trying not to lick the peach flavored lip gloss, but I'm hungry and the sweet taste is distracting. The makeup artist accepted the hundred dollar bill I slipped him in exchange for not painting me up so bad. Just some peachy bronzer on my cheeks and eyelids and gloss on my lips and I was done.

Mom walks by, giving me a hurried hug before some friend of hers pulls her away. I got all my looks directly from her and all my attitude directly from this oil tycoon standing before me.

"Okay. What's my agenda for tonight?" I scan the room and locate the buffet, knowing what I want my agenda to be.

"Socialize with the investors. And try playing pretty."

"I can't make any promises on that last part, sir." My nose wrinkles on its own accord as my newly plucked eyebrows pinch in disdain.

"Knock it off. I want a smile."

I can't help but present a goofy fake grin.

Shaking his head in defeat, Dad says, "You're a lost cause." With that he dismisses me into the crowd.

An hour later, I've managed to play pretty by keeping close to the food. I've had a few old geezers offer me their numbers with me politely declining. And most of the women I've spoken with only want to know who my stylist is and where my gold cuff and chandelier earrings came from—all of which I had to direct them to my mother. I have no clue. The only thing I do know is my red-soled shoes have the Louboutin label and every female in the room has been drooling all over them.

I've served my time, so my achy feet start easing closer and closer to the door. My hand is just a few feet away from freedom, aka the doorknob, when I hear Cooper call out from behind me.

"Samantha."

Reluctantly, I turn around and find he has a distracted Wiley Black in tow. I can't help but notice how his intimidating form fills out a black suit remarkably well. From the impeccably styled hair and neatly trimmed scruff, I'd be willing to bet his mom arranged a stylist attack on him, too. I've not encountered him closely without shades and a hat shrouding us both. My mouth dries as I take in the unobscured view of the very tall drink of water.

"Wiley, I'd like for you to meet my daughter, Samantha Shaw."

Wiley offers his hand along with an expression of confusion. "You look familiar."

Dad barks in laughter to my right, but I don't look at him. I'm too caught in the snares of mossy-green. Man, those babies are intense this close.

"She should. I believe you've ran into each other a few times on the field. Samantha is the head groundskeeper."

Wiley keeps shaking my hand, looking a little stunned. Without breaking eye contact with me, he mumbles, "You don't say."

Dad laughs some more, clearly enjoying the show. "Heard you put Sam in her place about watching your practice the other day."

Wiley seems to shake the haze of shock off as he says, "You'll have to forgive me for that, sir. I had no idea your princess was moonlighting as a maintenance worker."

"Black, my daughter is a lot of wonderfully exceptional things, but princess she is not."

Wiley's gaze wanders down to our clasped hands, honing in on my dirty nails. "No, sir. I suppose you're right about that." He joins Cooper—I refer to him as Cooper when I'm ticked or annoyed—in a round of raucous laughter, only irritating me further.

I yank my hand away and hide it behind my back. "If you two are done making fun of me, I'm calling it a night." The manicurist did her best earlier, and they were pristine until I arrived at the stadium and discovered a few wayward weeds in a flowerbed. I mean, I just couldn't have that. It's why I was late.

Before I can even take one step back, Cooper stops me. "Now wait a minute, young lady. How about congratulating Black on the win today."

Unimpressed, I motion toward Wiley. "You managed a win, albeit sloppy. Congrats." Turning on my red-soled heels, I strut out the door with as much attitude as my tired self can muster. I keep a clipped pace although I know one of the hotshots are following me.

As I reach the parking lot, a heated hand lands on my bare shoulder and spins me around. "What do you mean sloppy?"

I shrug his hand off and put some space between us. "If you're worth the seven figures I agreed to pay you, you should already know the answer to that."

You would have thought I physically struck him with the exaggerated flinch he produces. I think it's just sinking in about who I really am.

Taking a deep inhale and pushing it back out, Wiley pulls on his left earlobe. If I wasn't peeved at him, I'd find it endearing. "Look, I owe you an apology for how I've disrespected you in the last two months. If I would have known—"

"Whether I'm the head groundskeeper in my uniform or the co-owner of the Bobcats wearing a stupid dress, you should respect me the same."

"I know. Again, I'm sorry. But the team is my focus and I don't need any distractions on the field during practices."

"I can respect that. I don't want to cause your players any distractions."

"I'm talking about me."

That was unexpected. I didn't think I even showed up on his radar. "How can a 'kid' be distracting?"

"Sweetheart, the day we met, you felt yourself up in front of me. I've been distracted by you ever since." He leans closer, causing me to automatically take a step back.

"I patted my chest in sarcasm." I roll my eyes. I almost demonstrate the pat to make my point, but think better of it.

"I'm a man. Patting or feeling yourself up." He pauses to shrug his shoulders. "It's all the same. Besides, that sassing mouth of yours got under my skin just as much." His gaze looks heated and I take that as my cue to flee, but he intercepts me by clasping my arm. "How old are you?"

"It isn't polite to ask a woman her age." I know for a fact I'm older than his twenty-eight-year-old age—making him the youngest coach in pro-football history, thank you very much.

"You're of legal age though, right?"

"Depends on what you need me to legally do." I'm sassing, but from his dark expression, I've come off flirting instead. Embarrassed, I try bucking up with some attitude and say, "I've got a lot of work to do tomorrow and from today's game, you do, too. It's time to call it a night."

"About that. What's your take on it?" He's refusing to let go of my elbow.

Releasing a long sigh, I answer, "You have your hands full with Jones. He's like a fungus. If left untreated, he's going to infect your entire team."

He releases his own frustrated breath. "I know."

"I thought you had him straightened out, but from the looks of his head swelling on the field today…" I shake my head.

I use his grip on my arm to balance myself as I reach down and pull these ridiculous shoes off. Then with one firm yank, I free myself from his hold and head into the darkness.

"That's it? You're just going to leave?"

"Yes. I'm tired," I call over my shoulder while making a quick getaway towards the maintenance entrance. This dress isn't enough armor to keep myself in check in front of this man. Thank goodness, he doesn't follow me.

Chapter Five

I hear the ping echo through the early morning air before spotting Wiley on the fifty yard line. I pause to watch another ball zing through the air before it ricochets off the upright of the goal post and lands perfectly in a barrel. My focus is there so I don't see the unexpected ball heading in my direction until the last minute. My hands automatically reach out and grab it.

"Nice catch." His deep voice carries easily across the field as he takes a step in my direction. He's clad in the usual Bobcats T-shirt and track pants and no one has the right to make such meager clothing so appealing, but there he is doing just that. Man, is he tall and imposing.

I snap out of ogling him and sass, "Good thing I have attentive reflexes."

Instinctively, I send the ball back to him, triggering an impromptu game of toss and catch. Slowly, I ease farther on the field while we keep the ball whirling back and forth.

"Give me your take on Jones."

I'm guessing now that he knows I'm the hiring and firing part of the owner duo, Wiley gets that I know my stuff. Spiraling the ball back in his direction, I answer, "He's too young and immature to handle his new pro-football fame. My gut tells me he's going to be making headlines, and it won't be for his stellar football accomplishments."

He sends the ball back to me. "Me too. I've dealt with his kind all through my football days, just never from a coach's side of it."

"Have a 'Coming to Jesus' meeting with him. If that doesn't do the trick, bench him for a high profile game."

A smirk forms on his face. "That's the same advice your old man gave me."

"Smart man. Now stop pansying around and throw me some heat."

"You're too scrawny to handle it." He scoffs before sending back the ball.

"I can handle it, big boy. Show me what you got!" I taunt him.

"No."

"What? You can't bring it?" I keep taunting him and see it's working.

Pointing sternly at me, he warns, "You better catch it."

"Bring it on!"

And boy does he ever. The ball makes it to me before I can blink, but I'm still able to snag it. Fiery stings start in my fingertips and race viciously up my arms, sending me to the ground in withering pain. I try to holler out, but my voice has hightailed it and left only squeaky gasps behind.

I'm rolling on the field in pain when Wiley gets to me.

"What's the matter with you?"

There's teasing in his voice, but I don't reply. Can't. No voice. Yes, it hurts that bad! I think I must have caught a Mack truck running a hundred miles an hour on fire instead of a mere football!

"You need some ice, *baby*?" There's no sweet endearment in that last word. Nothing but pure mockery. He yanks me up like I'm a ragdoll and starts walking me toward the tunnel. And I let him, because all I want is for the throb of my poor hands to go away. This will be my last game of catch with Wiley Black.

"You asked for it, and I barely put any heat on it. *Wimp*." He's being way to smug about it.

The pain still has my voice captured, so I let him get away with it for now. He picks me up and places me on an exam table in the trainer's room before retrieving a bag of ice. I gladly take it when he offers the bag to me.

I'm finally able to stutter out, "That wasn't nice."

"You think the security cameras recorded it? It would definitely be a YouTube sensation." He has enough nerve to chuckle.

"Yeah. We could headline it 'Hermes hurts a poor kid' and your fans would turn on you in a heartbeat."

He hops on the table beside me. Well, more like sits down. His feet still can touch the floor for crying out loud. Mine are dangling.

"You do look like a kid, hiding behind those baggy clothes and big hat. I still can't get over what's really underneath."

"What are you talking about?"

Wiley reaches over and pulls my shades off. I can't defend myself, because both hands are clinging to the ice bag like it's a lifeline.

"That dress last night revealed it, and I'm glad these eyes of yours have been kept away from me until now. They're bewitching. I've never seen a blue so clear." Shaking his head, his mossy-green eyes study my blue ones with substantial intensity. "I can't believe you've not let me know who you really are in these last past months."

I'm getting flustered, so I go on the defense. "Look buddy, if you did your homework on the people signing your paycheck, you'd know who I am. I'm listed as Samantha Shaw, head groundskeeper and co-owner of the Texas Bobcats. It makes me question my judgement in vying so adamantly on your behalf to get this job."

A softness reaches his eyes. "You wanted me?"

I think Wiley is trying his hand at flirting, but I'm not buying into it. "As head coach for my team, yes. And just so you know, your parents recognized me immediately by just my name."

"You've met my parents?" His brows furrow.

Now that my hands are nicely numb, I hand the bag over to him. "Yep. We watched the game together yesterday."

Tossing the bag across the room and landing it perfectly in the sink with a satisfying *thump*, he mutters, "Unbelievable."

I'm not ready to go just yet, so I scan the trainer's room, inventorying for nothing better to do—steel ice baths, eleven more exam tables, three supply cabinets, four flat-screen TV's...

"Shaw. You married?"

"No." I glance at him and decide it's not wise, because something is obviously heating between us, so I focus on one of the dormant TV screens. "Shaw is my mom's maiden name. I don't want the notoriety that comes with Cooper. I'm grateful for what that name has achieved, but I want to make my own name for myself."

"That's impressive."

"No more impressive than you, Wiley Black."

His story still amazes me. On top of his game, Wiley was taken out with no chance of ever returning. Before he could get out of the hospital, his fiancée had the ring returned. The guy could have withered and went away. Instead, he hit rehab full throttle, spending all of his free time on the sidelines as an honorary coach the following season for his former team. He did whatever asked—forming plays, mentoring the replacement quarterback, you name it. And he did all this without receiving a dime for it.

That passion was all it took for me to become completely sold out on this guy. Life called a reverse on Wiley. He responded to the play the best he could and took off down the new route with guns-a-blazing.

The ticking hands of the wall clock grab my attention. "Ah shoot!" Jumping off the table, I run out the door. "I'm late. Catcha later," I holler over my shoulder without slowing down.

"Wait a minute," Wiley hollers back, but I don't have a minute so I keep trucking it until I reach my office upstairs.

I'm relieved to find Zane patiently sitting by my door. "Sorry about the holdup. Come on in." I push the door open and motion for him to follow me.

"No worries," Zane says as he accidently steps on the back of my shoe. "Sorry."

I wave it off and point to the chair opposite of my desk. After we're both seated, I get right to it. "About the logo you painted—"

"Yeah. It was epic. How'd you like the 3D effect?" His eyes light up in excitement.

"It was awesome. No doubt about it. But it's not the logo I gave you to paint."

Zane scratches the back of his head and looks a bit confused as to why that would matter. "So you didn't like it?"

"I loved it, but not sticking to the specifications the investors commissioned cost us a fine of ten thousand dollars." I pick up the invoice and show it to him.

His cute face goes slack. "Dude."

"Totally," I say, letting my inner hippie join him. "So, I have no choice but to suspend you for a week without pay." I pick up another paper and rummage for a pen before handing it over. "You also have to sign this agreement, acknowledging that you understand this is to never happen again or you'll be fired immediately."

"Sam, I'm sorry." He signs the paper and hands it back to me. Thankfully, he hasn't noticed my bright red palms. I'd hate to have to explain that.

"I know." I push a business card across the desk with the tip of my finger. "This was dropped off by the logo designer. I don't want to lose you, but I believe they will be offering you a better job."

"Wow... That's cool... But, Sam, can't I just stay here?" Zane is only nineteen with the entire world before him. I don't want to hold him back any more than I want to push him out in the midst of it before he's ready.

"Of course you can stay here, Zane. I selfishly want to keep you always, but the talent you have would be cheated if you didn't see what they are offering at least."

"Okay."

We both stand and I walk him out, before getting the day underway. It's already been a doozy.

*****

48

The week drags on with no excuse for it and I'm peculiarly antsy and don't know why. Everything has been trucking along as it should. There's no game to prep for this week, so the pressure is off, but the tension doesn't pay it any attention.

And at the moment, I'm not a happy camper at all. I've found myself in a place I declared I never would be caught. The men's bathroom. Luckily—if there's such a thing in this situation—this bathroom is only used by staff. And everyone has headed out for the day, so the embarrassment is kept just between me and these stalls. Donning rubber gloves up to my elbows, I go in for the attack. Knocking out the sinks first, followed by the urinals, I leave the stalls for last. Wielding the toilet cleanser and brush, I arm myself with a deep breath and proceed. Two sparkling toilets and a nose stinging from bleach fumes later, I ease into the last stall to wrap this up.

I'm in the midst of muttering all kinds of nasty things, when I hear the door bang open and then shut. Oh no… I was almost home free.

Bustling out of the stall, waving my handy-dandy-dripping toilet brush, I shout, "Whoa, whoa, whoa!"

None other than Wiley Black is standing before me in the process of unzipping his pants. He quickly sends the zipper back in its upright position, thank goodness!

"You trying to cause me to pee my pants?" he asks, stunned.

I lower my wet weapon. "No. Sorry."

"What are you doing?"

Shrugging my shoulders, I say, "I'm on bathroom duty."

A questioning smirk eases over his face. "How'd you manage that?"

"My after-hours janitor called in sick." I shrug again.

"Don't you have other staff?"

"They were all busy. Me and Colton flipped a coin. I lost." I shrug again. Colton said he would gladly take care of the bathrooms, if I agreed to go on a date with him. And that's a big fat no. He's a cutie with curly, light-brown hair and warm eyes to match, but he's too wild for my likings. In his mid-thirties, Colton could be running his own stadium, but he's too busy trying to be an eternal kid to muster enough gumption to do it.

Wiley chuckles. "You're the only billionaire I know who would be caught scrubbing toilets."

Before I can stop myself, both gloved hands hit my hips as I pin him with a glare. "My dad is the billionaire, and it doesn't matter if I'm the boss. I shouldn't ask any of my employees to do something I'm not willing to do myself."

Taking another step closer to me, making me have to crane my head back even more, Wiley openly stares as if he's trying to see more of me than ever before. It's just a plain canvas with no makeup and probably a few freckles, but he seems to think differently.

"Samantha Shaw, you are one unique woman," he says in a raspy whisper.

"Is that a good thing or a bad thing?" I squint at him.

The heat of his body caresses me he's so close now. "Definitely good."

Wiley's words cast a spell over me and all I can do is helplessly stare up at him. He finds an escaped wisp of my hair and tucks it back behind my ear. A lifetime passes in mere seconds before he clears his throat. "Sam."

Swallowing hard, I mutter, "Yeah?" I think the man is about to declare his love for me.

"I've really got to pee."

The reality of us standing in the midst of a men's bathroom comes back into sharp focus. I say nothing else and bolt for the door with cheeks blazing from embarrassment.

I put the cleaning supplies away, and call the day done.

Chapter Six

A football season is much more involved than the games on schedule. Press conferences, photo ops, interviews, and a menagerie of other high-profile events are all important factors. Tonight's event is being hosted by my parents out on the ranch and is for Wiley's charity foundation. It raises awareness about alcohol abuse in teens, and I'm proud to be a financial supporter of it.

My mom had a surprise attack of stylists pounce on me as soon as I arrived home an hour ago, so now I'm perfectly presentable and am driving the short drive to the main house. A girlie giggle escapes me as I think back over the last few weeks. The day after the crazy bathroom meeting, I received a text from an unknown number. The conversation went as follows:

Unknown – *Meet me for lunch.*

Me – *Who's this?*

Unknown – *Coach.*

I saved his number under Coach before replying.

Me – *How'd you get my #?*

Coach – *Did my H.W.*

The man put effort into tracking down my number, so I had to meet him for lunch after finding that out. We've been meeting up at the picnic area outside the stadium ever since. I was well aware already of the fact that Wiley Black is a stand-up guy, but I've enjoyed discovering he has a wickedly dry sense of humor. I find that very appealing. And he is just as dedicated to his players as I am with my crew. Just last week, the dad of one of his wide receivers passed away. Wiley dropped everything to fly out to Idaho with Timmons so the poor guy didn't have to make the trip by himself. He also remembers how to be just one of the guys. I enjoyed hearing about an impromptu water fight he participated in yesterday with the team after practice.

Speaking of practices, I'm still not allowed on the field during one. I've tested it and each time it earned me a stern head shake and crossed arms from Mr. Coach. So I've respected his wishes and watched from a suite instead. I like that he didn't change his rules after discovering who I am.

What's made me the happiest chick in southern Texas is him sitting with my family at church every Sunday for the last three weeks. He has only been a Texan for a couple months and he seemed really appreciative when I invited him. We have an early bird worship service, which is perfect for us ballgame folks. Wiley has even managed bringing along some of his players.

I arrive at the event in a peach gown, not minding it so much. It's long and flowy and the rich color of it is very complimentary. I don't even mind being a bit girlie tonight for a change.

I can't help but seek Wiley out as soon as I'm engulfed in the sea of formal wear. I find him immediately in the midst of what looks to be an intense conversation with a reporter. Never have I seen a black tux look so exquisite. My heartbeat quickens, but plummets even quicker when I notice a leggy redhead draped on his arm. Not wanting to chance running into them, I go hide out in my dad's game room. It's the size of a basketball court and is perfect to house the vast tables lined with goodies for the silent auction.

I try to ignore how it makes me feel that Wiley brought a date and focus on the reason for the night. I walk around a bit to scope out the goods. The place is packed with jovial people sporting deep pockets who are willing to empty them out a bit. And I'm counted as one of them, so I get on with it. My new plan is to drop a chunk of money, grab some food, and flee as fast as possible.

Thinking Delilah could use a spa day, I jot my name and a substantial bid down for a car detailing package. My girl deserves every penny. Moving on, I pass offerings for anything frou-frou and head straight to the table housing the concert package for Need to Breathe. I've seen these guys rock out at the stadium a few years back, and so I overbid to be sure in securing it. I want to offer the local schools a free concert next spring and these guys will be the perfect band. I move around and scribble my name and bids down for a dozen or so more items before I've done my part in the wallet portion of the night.

My stomach lets out a mean growl, so I follow my nose to the fiesta spread in the main dining room. It's been set up buffet style—my favorite. I've just grabbed a plate when I sense him behind me. Wiley has a way of towering over me protectively and so I know it's him without looking. For only knowing him a short time, it's odd how familiar he already feels to me. He trails behind me, piling his own plate, and maybe seeing what I have to say first. *Keep your eyes to yourself, Sam.*

Unable to stop myself, I blurt, "That's one gorgeous date you have tonight." His snort makes me break my rule and look at him—catching those mossy-greens rolling.

"My agent insisted a date would draw more attention to the event. He arranged it."

My gaze roams the room until it lands on his designated arm candy. "You have a wise agent."

"Yeah, but I could have been more creative than that." The heat of his words brush against my ear and sends a shiver along my neck. Abruptly, his arm snakes around my waist and draws me closer so that his lips are now touching my ear. "I can just picture the publicity I could get if I laid you across this table and claimed those peach lips... I can almost taste them."

My plate drops to the floor and shatters into millions of pieces. No. Not really, but WOW! The man just turned me into a hot mess of mush, and it's all I can do not to drop the plate. I have a strong urge to just melt into him.

Licking said lips that actually do taste like peaches, I let out a nervous laugh and try gaining some space from him by taking a step forward. "Nah. The picture would be much more vivid with your date sprawled across the table with all that flaming hair. If I saw that picture online or in a newspaper, there's no way I could pass up reading the article."

"I beg to differ." His deep raspy voice sounds strained a bit.

I adamantly will myself not to look at him while loading my plate with tamales—not knowing if my flustered belly will even accept food now that Wiley has it all stirred up with his sauciness. Did he really just suggest kissing me?

"Look, buddy. I think you need to knock off this flirting with me and mosey on back to your date."

A grunt sounds from behind me before he leans close to my ear again. "That's not an appealing option."

"Well, it's your only option. Good night."

I don't allow Wiley a rebuttal. Instead, I pull out of his grasp to make my way out. Dad is off to the side, and it's clear he's been watching the show from the wide grin spread on his face. I roll my eyes at him and head on out. I feel like a helpless prey trying to escape the forceful grasp of a predator. *Mercy*!

My feet only slow once my truck is in sight. It's not until now, do I realize I stole a plate of food. What's done is done, so I pull the tailgate down and have a private picnic under the clear night sky. The crickets chirping and the echo of a horse whinnying every so often in the distance keep me company and content. I've made it through a few tamales when the truck dips down beside me with a heavy weight. Yep. He's found me.

"Your folks go all out, don't they?"

I look over and find Wiley's head tilted back, studying the Edison-style lights dripping from the thick oak tree branches. "That's how they roll. Any given moment, ya know." I hitch a shoulder up, but he doesn't notice since he's still taking in all of the party décor. Woven amongst the lights, floral swags and gauzy material flutter about in the breeze.

He tilts his attention toward me. "What do you mean by any given moment?"

"It's an expression my dad uses all the time. Live each moment to the fullest, because at any given moment, it could be your last."

Wiley's lips curl up on one side. "Ah now. Sounds like the perfect reason for you to stop putting off giving me a kiss."

I shove into his solid shoulder. "Don't get fresh with me, mister."

Even though I try to deflect all the feelings this man is stirring in me with sass, the night air grows thick. A parade of fireflies wink across the pasture, so I take several deep breaths and focus on catching their little flashes of glowing green as a distraction.

"So this is your piece of junk that taunts all the guys each day at the stadium?" Wiley has enough nerve to steal one of my tamales *and* insult my truck. *The nerve of him.*

"How dare you talk about Delilah like that!" I swipe the tamale back just before he manages to pop it into his mouth.

"You named your truck?"

"My Paps named her. He was her first owner."

"I don't see anything feminine about this old truck." He looks at me skeptically and nods towards my girl.

"Well, neither am I."

"Oh, sweetheart. You're plenty feminine."

I don't know what to say to that, so I decide to deflect. "She'll take your prissy truck any day." Now I'm talking pure smack, because there's nothing prissy about his souped-up Ford F-150. I glance a few cars down from mine and spot the monster that is black on black on black. Even the rims, grill, and grill guard are black. But I'm not worried. I know what Delilah has under her hood.

"Is that a challenge?" Wiley asks as he does that leering thing again. I wonder when he's going to figure out that move has no effect on me.

Handing him the empty plate, I hop down. "You're on." I yank off the stilettos and toss them in the cab.

"Now?"

"Why not? There's a drag strip at the back of the ranch."

"Isn't that convenient."

"You chickening out on me, Coach?"

A mischievous grin lifts his wide lips. "Not on your life." Glancing at my exposed feet, he asks, "You're going to race me barefooted?"

"Heck no. Although I could totally kick your butt sans shoes. But tonight I'm gonna beat you wearing my boots." I pull them out of the cab, knock the dried grass clippings off, and settle back on the tailgate to lace them up. As I do this, Wiley starts working his tie off in preparation. We are both all business now.

"What's at stake?" he asks as he relieves a few buttons of his tux shirt.

"If I win, you give me back my access to the field any time I want."

Shaking his head, he says sternly, "No."

I pause in lacing my left boot to ask, "Well, why not?"

"I done and told you. You're too distracting."

I think about it and am coming up empty-handed. Especially when he untucks that shirt and allows me a sinful glimpse of his smooth defined abs.

"What? Are you going to race me naked?" I tease him.

Leaning so close, our noses graze. "Oh, I could totally kick your butt sans clothes, sweetheart. But tonight I'm going to beat you wearing a tux."

I'm beginning to think I'm blatantly playing with danger. It's as though I have no self-preservation at all. My heart revs up a few dangerous notches, sending my cheeks up in flames. Wiggling out of his grasp, I try coming up with what I want *when* I win. I could think of a few things, but they're not very ladylike...

An idea finally comes to me. "Hmm... If I win, I want you to clean the bathrooms for my guy one day next week."

Chuckling, he actually agrees with a nod of his head. "When I win, I want a taste of that peach lip gloss you're always teasing me with."

"*When*? Don't count your chickens before they hatch, Coach. Follow me."

Climbing into the cab of my truck, I inhale the comforting scent of sweet chewing tobacco and spicy Red Hots—the aroma belonging solely to my Paps. It is somehow permanently rooted in the leather bench seat. He had this truck totally rebuilt and then dressed it with a rusty frame full of character. I wanted it more than my teeth back in high school, so when graduation rolled around with Paps sadly not, he left it to me in his will.

Delilah and I bump along a back road, passing the horse barn and cow pasture until we reach the locked gate. Fishing the key out of the glove compartment, I jump out and take care of our only obstacle to getting to the drag strip. My dad and his buddies have ruined a car or ten out here, racing and causing ruckus. Honestly, I have, too.

Pulling up to the start, I hand roll down my window and listen as his passenger window whirls down smoothly. "We go on the count of three."

"Simple enough, Peaches." The dashboard lights show off a teasing gleam in his eyes.

Glaring over at him, I ask, "What did you call me?"

"Peaches. You're as pretty as a peach."

He's taunting me in hopes of flustering me. Not. Happening. I start the count while he's still laughing at himself. I yell three and gun it, sending dirt billowing all around. There's a vintage street light at the end of the strip, so I keep my focus there, daring no side glimpses.

Adrenaline courses through me, releasing an excited, "Woohoo!" But I tamp it down a notch when the black monster starts to ease up next to Delilah. Foot to the pedal, I manage to hold him off from passing me.

It's recklessly over before I know it, with me barely claiming the win. Both trucks fishtail to a stop, engulfing us in a cloud of dust. After it settles back down, I jump out to do a victory dance with Wiley's headlights as my spotlight. Twirling around and doing a little shimmy, I let go and live in the triumphant moment. I'm having myself just the largest time, when I notice he's still in the truck and not making a move to get out. I stop and hold my hand over my eyes, trying to shoo the light away enough to peer in at him. It's no use. Everything is too dark.

"What's the matter? You a sore loser?" I yell out.

After what feels like a millennium, he finally steps out of his truck. He looks at me in a confused awe, which is confusing me.

"What?" I ask, backing up. He's got that predator stance again, and it's making me nervous. *Flight or fight* races through me.

He doesn't speak. Instead, he grabs me up and places me on the hood of my truck. With his hands placed on each side of my hips on the hood, Wiley leans down to study me. He's looking at me like I'm some complicated math problem and is debating whether I'm worth the time it'll take to figure out.

"What?" I ask again.

"There are just too many facets to you, Peaches. I'm warming to the idea of talking you into letting me explore each one a little closer." The crisp scent of his cologne engulfs me as he leans even closer.

"But... I won," I stutter out like an idiot.

"I know, but I really want to taste that lip gloss." His nose skims along mine, as he waits for permission.

I can't help but lick my lips and taste the peach flavor still clinging to them. That's some really good stuff. I'm so flustered, I have to take several calming breaths.

After regaining my composure, I set out to tease him. "I might be able to afford you a small taste," I whisper.

"I'll take whatever you're willing to give." His voice comes out hoarse and the hammering of his heart flutters against my palm—I don't even recall placing it on his chest.

I press my index finger along my lips and swipe with hopes of collecting some of the lip gloss before shoving it in his mouth. I've done it with goofing off in mind, but it backfires instantly when he captures my finger between his teeth and starts rolling his tongue along it. We both release a groan and my mouth waters to taste *him* now.

I'm ready to give in and allow him a kiss, when he abruptly releases me and walks back to his truck. "Good night, Peaches," he hollers before shutting his door and driving off.

What. Just. Happened?

"Argh!"

Wiley Black just snatched my little play of power and drove off with it. I plop back on the hood and scold myself for allowing my guard down enough to let him steal the upper hand.

Chapter Seven

The fall is falling around us, but this southern state is still clinging on to some of its warmth. All is well in the Bobcat world. Sort of... They've won all games so far, but one. And that one game resulted in Jones instigating a fight on the field. The two games following, he has been sulking on the bench and not allowed to dress. I shake my head on that mess and shuffle through the papers on my desk.

"Knock, knock!" Mom's voice chimes out by the door. "Lunch!"

I look up and see she's waving a nice-sized Renata's takeout bag. Spicy aroma greets me and sets my mouth to watering. I pushed a spreader all morning and I'm starved. Only problem with this set up is I already have lunch plans. Glancing at the clock, it reminds me that it's to be commencing in ten minutes. No way will Mom be out the door that fast.

"Hey, Mom. That smells heavenly." I shoot Coach a quick text, letting him know Mom's visiting me. He's taken up calling me Peaches and so I only call him Coach now. Sometimes I throw in Jerk for good measure. Shoving the paperwork back in the intake tray, I pat the cleared desk expectantly.

Mom rewards by laying out boxes filled with chicken tacos and lots of guacamole. Have I mentioned I have the best mom ever? I look up at her and see the few greys she had peppering through her black hair last week have magically disappeared. She could pass for my sister. And she's vibrant enough to pass as my *younger* sister.

"So, my sweet darlin', how's life treating you?" she asks after gracing our food.

Cramming a hefty bite of taco in, I mumble out, "Good. No complaints." I notice she's eyeing me in hopes of obtaining more, but I'm not giving it. Cooper's been running his mouth, so I know good and darn well this is about Wiley Black.

My phone dings a new message. Looking down where it's resting in my lap, I read —*Just got an unexpected lunch invite from Cooper.*

"So, where did you disappear to the night of the event at the ranch?"

That was a few weeks back. Why now? "What's your game, Mom? Just spit it out." I run my last bite through the thick guacamole before popping it in my mouth.

"Your dad found the gate at the back of the property unlocked yesterday. Checking the security camera, he found something pretty interesting."

"Ugh!" That man and his security cameras! I thought I took care of that particular one at the drag strip with a few *accidentally* thrown rocks. "I'm thirty years old come next week. I can race if I want." Tossing the wrappers in the bag, my appetite has fled out the door and I sure wish I could follow it.

"And you're old enough to make out with a man, too."

I look up and find her light-blue eyes twinkling. I'm guessing the race wasn't the *interesting* part. Oh boy. I wonder if Cooper is stringing Wiley up by his feet as we speak. I send him a one word text—*SORRY*.

"We're just friends, Mom... And that night we were goofing around... And I don't think it's a good idea to get too close to him... I don't like to get close to the players and coaches... And—" I'm rambling on and on in nervousness.

"I think that 'getting close' part is null and void, sweetheart. And sometimes you can't help it." She's just a smiling as she cleans up our lunch.

"Mom..." I whine, not knowing what else to say.

Kissing my cheek, she says, "I'm going to go snoop out the haunted trail. I'll see you later. Love you, darlin'."

"Love you, too."

After Mom has left me with way more than I want to think about, I find something to do to get my mind off of it. I pull out the papers again to sign off that all safety precautions have been met for the haunted trail. Cooper Stadium has a very talented special events coordinator. Christina sets up all of the concerts and rodeos that take place off season. And she comes up with some fun events during the season.

This year, Christina has transformed our vendor corridor into a small carnival with a haunted trail to help celebrate the spooky season. It's going to be a great family-fun activity and it's set to open tonight.

Loyal Zane has stayed on with us and I hate he blew off that job opportunity with the logo design company. But I'm grateful to still have him, so I approached Cooper about giving him a raise. That only raised his eyebrows in indignation. I know the guy cost us ten grand, but I won't give up until the big guy caves. I was able to get Zane commissioned to do all of the design and painting for the haunted trail. I've only seen bits and pieces so I'm pretty excited to see the finished product later.

Later on, my phone alerts a new message as I hand over the paperwork to Cooper's assistant.

Coach – *I'm still alive.*
Me – *Lucky you.*
Coach – *Make it up to me by having dinner with me.*
Me – *IDK. Weirdos are going to be out tonight.*
Coach – *Yes or no?*
Me – *Maybe.*
Coach – *Always so stubborn.*

I leave him stewing for a while. The haunted trail has been open for an hour now, and I want to take a peek. I brush the few remaining grass clippings off my shirt and pants and call it done before heading downstairs.

The entire lobby is packed with folks waiting their turn. Wow. Christina has outdone herself on this one. Vendors have perfumed the area with freshly popped kettle corn, candy apples, and cotton candy. Grabbing up a bag of the popcorn, I take a spot in line. Munching and moving for the next little bit, I'm going over the game day schedule for tomorrow when a giant gremlin sidles up beside me. Well, more like a guy wearing a gremlin mask with his black hoodie covering his head.

"You're still going to get recognized, Coach." I snort before shoving another handful of salty-sweet goodness in my mouth.

His hand darts out to cover my mouth. "Shh..."

Pushing it away, I offer him some of my treat. "Want some?" It's then when I realize there's no mouth opening. Laughing, I pop another handful in my mouth.

"You're not funny." His voice is muffled and he sounds kinda cute.

"Oh, yes I am." I wave my ID—my co-owner one—to the ticket collector. "This oversized gremlin is with me."

"Yes, Miss Shaw." The young guy smiles as he waves us in.

The place is pitch-black for a few beats until we reach a tunnel. All of a sudden we are in a section of vibrant art depicting ghosts and goblins in neon being lit up by black lights. I can't believe this is our vendor corridor. All identity of it has been completely replaced with a vivid haunt. Wiley has placed his hand protectively on the small of my back and I could almost swear that part of my body was created just for him to do that. I try not to get too lost in the warmth of his contact and beckon my feet to keep moving forward. The next section we enter, a cool breeze hits me and we are now walking through a graveyard. Ghostly sounds float around us as we inspect the gloomy place.

Laughing, I point to the headstones. "All the teams you've whooped this season."

A bitter chuckle sounds from under his mask. "There's a headstone missing."

Wiley is still sore from that one loss. "Get over it already, Coach."

Shoving me in the side, he barks, "Stop calling me that."

People are too busy checking out everything to be paying us any attention. I shrug my shoulder and keep going until a blond zombie jumps out of one of the tombs and grabs me up.

"Brains!" Zombie growls as I flail around screaming, nearly losing my bag of popcorn.

After the section empties with the spectators fleeing in terror, Zombie Zane hands me back over to the gremlin.

"Awesome job, Zane."

"Thanks, dude." He hurries back to his position with no time to spare on chitchatting.

"He just called you dude?" Wiley muffles out.

"Yeah. Would you rather he call me *sweet thang*?" I can't help but tease.

"Dude is fine." He says this too quick and sounding a bit jealous. I think I like that fact too much.

After my heart slows its pace back to normal, we walk through to the next part. A mad scientist is hopping around a waking Frankenstein once we reach it. The monster snarls and lunges at a few spectators, but keeps just out of arms reach. One of the rules is to not touch anyone, but I'm guessing I'm the exception to the rule for tonight. Once again, I find myself grabbed up in the snares of a monster—this time by Frankenstein, who is declaring me his bride. Eventually, he returns me to my gremlin, who grouches something about people needing to keep their hands to themselves. I can't wipe the grin off my face at his possessive tone.

The fun continues for ten fun-filled minutes before we emerge outside in the cool night.

Yanking the mask off, Wiley reveals he's washed down in sweat. I can't help but run my hand through his damp hair to unplaster it from his forehead.

"That thing is hot," he comments while leaning down slightly to allow me a better reach.

As I do this, he pulls my hat from my head and returns the gesture. "How do you manage hiding all of this hair under that hat every day?"

My eyes roll to the back of my head from the massaging of his fingers on my scalp. "Very carefully," I slur.

He takes a step forward and I'm about to venture resting my head on his abdomen—because that's as close to his chest as I can reach—when a bunch of kids scream out in excitement.

"It's Hermes!"

And that, my friends, concludes the moment.

Wiley is surrounded in seconds and is signing autographs before I can blink.

He glances at me and scoffs playfully. "See. When you're around I get distracted. This is your fault."

I shake my head in protest and witness him interact with these kids. He's such a good sport about it until the group bloats out to adults and lots of them. I send a security alert out and have him rescued within thirty minutes. Before he can wiggle completely free with help of a few bodyguards, I head out. It's already late and we both have a big day tomorrow.

*****

Game day goes off without a hitch. The guys pull out a win and Jones actually behaves himself for a change. Lots of celebrating and fun takes place all afternoon and well into the evening before the stadium finally quietens for the night.

Although the game wrapped several hours ago, the energy of the win still crackles the air in exhilaration. Covered in goose bumps, I'm reveling in it

After pulling on a Bobcats hoodie and checking the security report that states the stadium is successfully locked down for the night, I make my way back to the field. It's pitch-black with hardly any moon to light my way, but I could make it to centerfield blindfolded. Dropping to a seated position and then lying back, I allow my fingers the luxury of testing the abused turf. I love how resilient it is. What other living thing could withstand such an assault as today's game and still be vibrant with life?

As my fingers play through the soft blades of grass, I take in the view of the star-dusted sky. They are magically twirling around the crescent moon and my breath catches at the magnificence of it. God is one brilliant artist. No doubt about it. This painting whispers a reminder to me of how small I am in the whole scheme of life.

The only sounds are the slight whooshing of a light breeze playing through the stands and the far-off buzz of city life. An unfamiliar sound interrupts the melody, causing me to stiffen in panic—harsh footsteps coming close. All I can do is lift my head and try to find the point of danger.

"I'm calling the cops so it's best you hightail it on out of here," a deep voice shouts.

Relief rushes over me instantly. Setting my head

back down, I say, "It's okay. I have a key. And the security code. And I know a few secret exits."

"Sam?"

"Wiley."

I sense before seeing him come to a halt beside me, but pay him no mind by keeping my attention on the night sky. His body heat reaches out and warms the length of my right side as he lies down next to me. His freshly washed scent pairs well with the sweet scent of the grass, so I greedily take several deep inhales of it.

"I'm beginning to worry you live here." He nudges my side.

"I could easily say the same about you."

"Touché."

"No victory party tonight, Coach?"

"I'm sure the boys are living it up, but that's not my scene."

I keep testing the texture of the grass as I say, "Partying never was your scene, was it?"

"How'd you know that?"

"How many times do I have to tell you I've done my homework?"

"Boxers or briefs?" His question presents as a challenge.

"Boxer briefs, if your Calvin Klein contract is accurate. You're trying to change the subject."

"No. No partying for me. I watched my buddy die from alcohol poisoning at the only party I attended in high school. We were out at some

73

dilapidated barn and couldn't figure out how to get an ambulance to us." A deep, uneven sigh escapes him.

My thoughts linger on his foundation as we fall in a silence. No wonder he advocates the awareness of alcohol abuse with such dedication. Something as devastating as that has to leave an everlasting mark. After a while, I try to lighten up the subject or at least throw it down another track.

"How was your lunch date with Cooper yesterday?"

A deep rumble of laughter emits from him, and so I smile at knowing I chose right. "Great. He fed me a perfectly-cooked porterhouse steak while explaining to me if I hurt you in any way, he will have me castrated."

"Smart man," I say through a bout of giggles.

"You've got a standup old man."

"I know. I'm very blessed."

"How long do you plan on staying out here?" He pops up long enough to pull his hoodie over his head before lying back down. It's just slightly nippy, but I've already got my hoodie up to ward off the faint chill.

"I don't set a time limit. An hour... All night..."

"And why are you out here?"

"This is how I celebrate a home win."

"By lying on the fifty-yard line?"

I look over at him and can barely make out the line of his profile in the darkness. "It's my way of

74

congratulating the field for doing its job for the game." He doesn't comment so I continue on with my philosophical game view. "This game of football goes beyond the player roster and the coaches. This field, the stadium, the maintenance and janitor staff, the owners and investors, the vendors, and most importantly the fans... So many parts working together to honor this grand American sport." Somewhere in the midst of my speech, Wiley's hand finds mine and warms it in his grasp. It's such a luxury, so I decide to let him keep it.

"Wow. My eyes pricked at that speech, Peaches."

I go to tug my hand free, but he won't allow it. "Don't make fun. You know it's true."

"Absolutely. Every word."

My heart picks up in speed as his thumb absently traces a circle near my wrist. When he stills, I roll over and place my head on his chest and melt when he wraps his arm around me.

"Wiley?"

"Yeah?"

"Will you tell me why you've stayed in the game?"

Tugging my hood down, his fingers slowly work through my tangles. "Football is all I know. Life called an audible and I had no choice but to accept it."

"Humph. The reverse is my favorite play analogy. Life can change direction and you have no choice but to alter your game plan and follow."

"True... I'm just happy I was able to eventually

walk away. Too many other injuries occur on this field where players don't get that option. I'm blessed."

Eventually Wiley works the tension away as he rhythmically runs his fingers through my hair, settling my heartbeat into contentment. We talk of life and football and of life some more, until I notice the sky's dark hue turns softer and we succumb to sleep…

The sun is bright and assaulting and my eyes refuse to open.

"Sam."

I ignore Trey and snuggle into the warm cocoon surrounding me. Everything fades back to the void of delicious sleep for not nearly long enough, when I hear Trey's annoying voice disrupting it again.

"Sam."

Trey? The fuzz evaporates instantly, forcing me to jolt up. I'm not in a bed surrounded by a down comforter. Blinking back to reality, I find myself smackdab in the middle of the football stadium, damp from the dew with a giant quietly snoring beside me.

"You've got less than five minutes before people start arriving." I squint up at Trey and find him trying to hide a grin.

Pushing frantically on Wiley's thick shoulder, I say, "Hey. We've got to get going. Now!"

Gathering himself in a seated position, Wiley

releases a long yawn. Looking around groggy-eyed with his dark hair sticking in all directions, he seems to be working on figuring out where he's at. It suddenly registers on his face as he stands up and starts limping towards the tunnel, muttering who knows what all the way. I cringe at the pronouncement of his limp, guessing the field must not have set well with his leg. I make note not to repeat this with him for that fact.

Trey snickers as I dust off the grass and head for the exit.

"Don't say a word," I mutter in warning.

"It's going to cost you," he says with tease lacing his tone.

"How much?"

"I mow the field this week."

"Fine," I say.

"Wow. It must be worth a lot to you."

I look over and find his eyebrow raised, challenging me to rebuke him. The thing is, he's right. Wiley Black is becoming worth a lot more to me than that paycheck I sign.

Leaving Trey in the bay, I head for my office. Luckily, it has a full-sized bathroom attached so I can grab a quick shower. Of course, I have an entire wardrobe stashed, too. I'm beginning to think Wiley isn't too far off about me living here.

I place a quick phone call to Dad's assistant and ask her to have breakfast delivered to the coach's office, knowing Wiley has staff meetings set to start in only minutes. I'm feeling generous so I go ahead and order breakfast for my guys too, before I hit the shower.

The afternoon wears on and I can barely keep my eyes open. I've just sat on a golf cart to rest my eyes for a minute when my phone goes off to the beat of the Jaws theme song. I hit ignore twice before *duuun dun duuun dun dun dun dun dun* starts driving me crazy again.

"Yes," I mumble after hitting accept.

"My office. Now." With that Cooper hangs up.

Shoving my tired body off the cart, I drag my feet all the way upstairs. The door to my office beckons as I pass it, but my feet reluctantly keep on to the path to dad's office. From the unyielding tone of his voice on the phone, he won't be allowing me to stand him up today. Pushing the door open, I find my mother sitting in Dad's lap like she's a love-struck schoolgirl.

"All right, Jenny, there's four perfectly good chairs in this room. Pick one." Since she's acting like a kid, I thought I would try parent on for size. From the look of her face, she's about to reclaim her rightful role.

"And you have three perfectly good beds at your home. You should pick one of those to sleep in, instead of the football field."

That's all it takes for me to throw my hands in the air and slowly start backing out of the room, not wanting to rile up Momma Bear any further.

"Get back in here," Dad says. The sternness of his

command has me back in and plopping down in one of those chairs I was just pointing out to Mom.

"I can't even pick my nose without the two of you knowing about it." I huff and focus on my green stained hands. I sprayed the field this morning and the colorant of the chemical spilled into my fatigued hands instead of in the tank.

"I think it's sweet how that boy is courting you." Mom's voice drips with honey. I roll my eyes because I don't really think any *courting* is going on.

Looking up, I notice Dad isn't as sweet on the idea as Mom. He's all pinched eyebrows and she's all dreamy-eyed. And I'm all embarrassed.

"We didn't mean to fall asleep out there. And no one but Trey saw... Well, you two did, too. I think you need to just step away from the security monitors, Dad. Seriously, I'm not your reality TV show."

He holds his hand up. "Sam, just be careful. I've always thought it was wise of you to keep your distance from the team. But now you're blurring your code, and I worry you're going to get hurt."

I try rubbing the irritation from my eyes and it's all I can do to pry them back open. "I know. I'll be careful. Nothing has happened that I wouldn't be able to walk away from."

There's a punctuated lull in the conversation, so I take the opportunity to walk away from this uncomfortable discussion. I'm surprised when they both actually allow me. I shuffle down the hall and am startled with who I find sitting behind my desk like he owns the joint. Taking a moment to just appreciate him being in my space, I decide he looks good there, so I let him keep that chair. I'd rather have the leather couch by the wall anyway.

Plopping facedown, I ask, "How's your leg?"

"Good. Had one of our trainers work on it for a while. Nice office, by the way."

"Seems you've made yourself at home," I mumble as I turn my head to peek at him. I notice he's grabbed a change of clothes along the way, too. His track-pants-clad legs are propped on my desk, looking right comfortable. I enjoy the view until my eyes drift shut...

"Sam."

"What?" The grouch is prominent in my voice, but I'm too tired to soften it.

"You started snoring."

"Then why'd you wake me?"

I'm about to doze back off when his big ole body tries to fit on the couch with me. Good thing it's a sizable couch. And the cocoon that I enjoyed very much this morning is back. Ahh... "Just what are you doing?"

"I'm sleepy, too." Nuzzling into the side of my neck and taking in a deep inhale, he rasps in a tired voice, "Mmm... You smell good."

I scoff. "Do not. I smell like dirt."

"I know. Smells good on you." Wiley takes another deep inhale, causing a tingle to skirt along my neck. "Samantha Shaw. You're starting to control my clock." His warm lips press a kiss to my neck before I drift off.

I dream about scoreboards and timeclocks ticking down.

Chapter Eight

As with any season, when you find it going exactly as planned, you can just about guarantee a trick play is going to come out of nowhere and turn everything on its blame ear. We weren't immune and everything got thrown off. Wiley was beyond stressed with the media breathing down his neck over Jones getting out of control and bringing a few other players down with him. So with two game losses and the hopes of the playoffs dwindling, I felt it was *time* for a timeout.

My birthday tag from last week draws my attention as I wait for Wiley to arrive in my office. It's a beautiful sign created by Zane himself with the guidance of my beloved crew. I trace the swirling three and then the zero. I had no idea I had it pinned to my back all day until Wiley of all people pointed it out. "Thirty Year" at the top of the sign with "Old Maid" underneath it in metallic black and gold. Even lovelier than that was when Wiley pointed out, in front of most of my crew, that I am actually older than him. I already knew that, but everybody else didn't need to know it, too.

I forgave him for that when he whisked me away to Renata's later that evening for a birthday supper — just the two of us. After concluding the meal with delicious fried ice cream, he presented me with a custom license plate. It has a royal-blue background with 'Delilah' painted in gold cursive script. It sure is fancy for my old girl, but even in the sea of rust it suits her. There's no way not to swoon over a man that thoughtful.

"Hey."

I look up and find the handsome devil standing at my door. "Hey. Come on in." I motion for him to have a seat. "How'd practice go?"

Plopping down in the chair, Wiley scrubs his hands down his tired face. "It went." There's no confidence in his voice, so I know what I'm about to enforce is in his best interest.

"I've got you scheduled to take off Monday through Wednesday next week."

"Cancel it. I've got too much mess going on here."

"No can do. It's set. You need a break. Take it."

Leaning over his knees, he says, "No." His expression is hard and challenging.

I challenge right back. "You will. Or I'll officially suspend you those days."

"You can't be serious?" His eyes go wide in disbelief as he sits back.

"I am, so please don't test me." I raise my hand to stop him before he can protest. "You're burnt out, Wiley. Take the three days and get some rest."

Shaking his head, he repeats, "No."

Well, hotshot didn't want to do this the easy way—big surprise. Yes, insert a whole lot of sarcasm and eye-rolling here. This man and I should get an A+ in the butting-heads category. So an hour later, I have the suspension paper drafted and am presenting it to him to sign.

"You've forced my hand, you stubborn man." I grit each word out, just as mad about this as he is.

Wiley signs with so much force that the paper actually tears in places. Boy is he mad. I've never seen anger paint his handsome face red before until now.

Minutes later, the notary hands me and Mr. Ornery a copy of the paper before she scurries away from the thick tension in my office. Wiley won't look at me, so I ease around the desk and make myself comfortable in his lap.

"Don't be mad at me," I whisper, pulling his face in my direction until he finally blesses me a glimpse of his green eyes.

"I am." Something flickers through those gorgeous peeps, maybe a last-ditch idea. "I'll let you back on the field any time you want. Even during practices."

"Too late. You've already signed. Now I want you to pack a bag and be ready to pull out by six Monday morning."

"What are you talking about now, woman?" A growl releases from the depths of his chest.

"We have a lake house in Tyler. I want you to spend your suspension there."

"What? I didn't agree to that." He's literally pouting—lips poked out and everything.

"Actually, you did. What idiot signs his name to something before reading it thoroughly?" I scoff.

Wiley reaches around me and plucks the document off my desk and starts skimming it. "Samantha." My name comes out in a grumble and so I'm guessing I'm Samantha to him when he's ticked off. He halfheartedly pushes at me to get off his lap, but I latch on.

"Tyler is only two hours away. You won't be that far. Stop pouting about it and look at the potential."

"Potential?"

I try smoothing his pinched brows back apart with my fingertip. "I'm spending all day Monday with you." I offer this, even though I'm not sure it's an appealing proposal to him at this point.

He seems to be thinking things over and a lopsided smile finally forms on his lips. "You have to promise to wear the peach lip gloss."

"Done."

"And you have to promise I'll get to taste it."

"Done."

"From your lips this time." His pinched eyebrows relax as one lifts with authority. That's my guy. As long as he feels he has the upper hand. Whatever the big guy needs.

"That's probably doable."

"Not good enough of an answer." His words are presented in that coach's voice of his.

"Done."

"It most certainly is." The wild glint in his eyes confirms I may be in a whole lot of trouble.

*****

Arriving to a chilly November day at the lake with no cloud in sight, my own tension dissolves and disappears in the crisp air. I park beside Wiley's black monster and meet him on the front porch. After we enter, I march him straight to the master bedroom to take care of some important business. And he's all game until he figures out we have different game plans.

"Why?" His hands are perched on his lean jean-clad hips. He doesn't wear jeans often enough in my opinion. The man definitely knows how to wear a pair *well*.

We keep having a standoff, with Wiley having no intentions of giving over his cellphone.

"You're suspended from it, too. But don't worry. All of the numbers you could possibly need are on a card by the house phone. I even called your mom and gave her the house number." I wiggle my fingers palm side up, waiting for him to relent. He finally does and places the phone in my awaiting hand. Powering it down, I lock it in the house safe hidden in the closet.

"What if my team or staff needs me?" He's all but whining.

"You'll be contacted in emergencies only. Call me Wednesday before you leave and I'll give the combination for the safe."

Folding his arms over his broad chest, he glares down at me. "I'm still not happy with you."

"You're allowed. Now how's about we get your mind off things." I head for the door, but find myself locked in his arms.

His lips touch the tip of my ear before he speaks. "I can think of something that'll get my mind off things."

Laughing nervously, I wiggle out of his grasp. "Your momma says she's raised a perfect gentleman. Don't go proving her wrong. Now behave." I head straight through the house and out the back door with Wiley hot on my heels. Thank goodness, we are both in thick sweaters and jeans. The wind has quite a sharp nip to it today.

"I think we've danced around long enough, Peaches. I want a kiss."

"Well, demanding it like that isn't very romantic." My nose wrinkles and my eyes squint in disapproval as I give him a sidelong glance.

"I didn't take you for being a romantic kind of girl." He smirks.

"Try again later. You've ruined the mood, buddy." I lead him down the pier and to the end where a few Adirondack chairs await us. Sitting down, I motion for him to join me.

"This is it? We're sitting?" He grunts a few beats as though he finds the chair unappealing. "I'm not a sitting around kind of guy."

"I know, but you can hold my hand while you give it a go." I offer my hand and he secures it in his calloused yet gentle grasp.

The view is exquisite with the vast body of dark water undulating softly and the trees surrounding it protectively. We watch a group of lazy turtles get lapped by a bustling crowd of ducks. They squawk at the turtles, but the lethargic creatures pay them no mind.

It's fairly quiet this time of year and peaceful. I settle in and mellow out. Unfortunately, my antsy guest only lasts ten minutes before he is up and moving. We end up walking the shoreline a majority of the day, but I still consider it a success when I witness his bunched-up shoulders relax and the scowl on his face replaced with a contented smile.

I think the combination of the calming lake and being completely unplugged from the electronic world is the reason for that smile. It's like obtaining an exclusive pass to just *be*. And nothing more.

I called ahead and had the kitchen stocked with food, so I busy myself with grilling some chicken and veggie kabobs for an early supper. There are huge picture windows in the living room, so I exiled Wiley there to try relaxing some more. He wasn't so crazy about not finding a TV in the house. After piling two plates full, I walk them out to the living room where I find the larger-than-life man passed out cold.

I place the plates on the coffee table and just admire him for a while. I'm guessing the man doesn't get many opportunities to just unwind. With his head resting on the back of the tall couch, a relaxed expression has softened his chiseled features. I could just stand here and take in the view, but my fingers itch to participate as well.

After debating a few seconds, I give in and sit beside him. I reach out and gently test the scruffy yet appealing dark stubble on his cheek with my fingertips. I didn't see myself growing attached to him, but it's happened anyway. Even his bossiness draws me to him. I can't explain it. And honestly, that's why I've not allowed him a kiss yet. Just as soon as I do I know I'll be a goner, but the yearning to experience that connection with him has become overwhelming.

I don't have much experience in the kissing department. Most guys I've dated ended up being intimidated by my dad or salivating at the mouth over him. Neither group is appealing in the least and ended up just being a big hassle. But this man sleeping in front of me is such a different story. I have a feeling Wiley Black would be worth any hassle presented. My main worry is that I'll disappoint him.

The nervous tremor of my hand ebbs as my fingers softly thread through his thick locks. The hue is so dark, it's close to black. Wiley is still out cold, so

I scoot a little closer until our breaths mingle and pause there a while to build up some courage. I whisper my lips across his and the world tilts when his eyes open, and I'm instantly captured by the power in that stare. His strong arms lock around me and gently tug until I'm completely on his lap.

Holding each other's gaze, our lips softly meet again—testing and exploring in a languid pace. It's so tender and slow and has set an ache so dangerously sweet that my body shivers. Wiley leads this kiss and when he lightly beckons my lips to part with his own, all I can do is follow.

We explore the depths of this kiss with no timeclock ticking down with demanding we hurry. There's nothing to hold us back and his firm grip on my waist wouldn't allow me to flee even if I wanted to. But I don't want to flee. Not even a little.

Nothing has ever felt so right, yet so scary. It's like I just nosedived off a terrifyingly-steep cliff, but find myself landing in a soft fluffy cloud of serenity. I would almost swear to the fact that my lips were created to do nothing but kiss this man. This is so new and delicious and all-consuming.

As with any moment in time, it must come to an end. I reluctantly release Wiley's lips and press my forehead against his so that I can catch my breath. The strong rising and falling of his chest indicates he's in need of air, too.

"I'd like nothing better than to have your sweet lips wake me up for the rest of my days, Peaches." I think he added Peaches to downplay the seriousness of the statement he just proclaimed. I'm not a girlie girl who's going to get all flustered and overanalyze his words, but *for the rest of his days* is a really long time...

"I'm sorry," I say, before moving my lips to the warmth of his neck. When they explore the tender skin behind his ear, I feel a shiver race through him and hear a deep rumble escape his throat.

"Why?" Wiley asks, his voice husky.

"I forgot to put on my peach lip gloss."

Cupping my chin so that I sit back up and look at him, Wiley says, "Baby, that kiss couldn't have gotten any sweeter." There's no doubt that *baby* is an endearment this time, and I like it too much.

"I don't know... Maybe we should try it with the lip gloss to be sure..." I pull the tube of gloss out from my pocket and we give it a good go. And just let me tell you, kissing this man can only get sweeter.

Chapter Nine

The offense has forty seconds to snap the football. *Only* forty seconds. Decisions have to be made and there's no going back on them once they're made. There's just no time for second-guessing. And no matter what happens once that ball is snapped, the players have to follow through and endure any consequences of that choice.

Leaving Wiley at the lake house was a decision I felt comfortable with and was proud I followed through with it. Arriving back to my office late Monday night, another decision challenged against the timeclock with no room for second guessing. Could I have done it differently? Yes. Millions of other moves have taunted me. But what's done is done and now the consequences…

The consequences are divvying out as Wiley's fists slam a locker viciously, causing the entire locker room to ring out in loud shrills of his anger. The place is abandoned due to an emergency meeting being called. The players got an unexpected day off until we can calm Wiley down.

"You left me in the dark on purpose. That's the whole reason you ordered me to Tyler. To be out of your way!" Wiley's fist lands another blow to the locker door, the metal screeches in protest. I'm thinking I was stupid instead of brave for volunteering to tell him.

"That's ridiculous. I had no idea about the offer until I got back late Monday night." I take a deep breath and proceed a little calmer. "You know as well as I do, a trade window starts closing as quickly as it opens. It was a wise decision and I don't regret it."

Crossing his arms, Wiley peers down at me with his face painted a violent shade of red. "This is my team and it's my right to know about trades or anything else you *owners* choose to pull on *my* boys."

"Jones was a ticking time bomb and you know it. You owe it to Grant to have the best offensive line. You wouldn't want to fail him the way your coach failed you." I have an urge to shove him, but tamp it down.

"Don't bring me up in this."

It may not be very wise, but I push forward anyway. A point needs to be made. "Those three guys had no business on the field that day. They were still drunk and dangerously dehydrated. Your coach must have known—"

"Enough!" The one word growls out so ferociously, it makes me flinch. Muttering a few choice words, Wiley storms out.

My legs give out, so I slide to the floor and rest

my head against the locker. This is why I don't get close. It's my responsibility to make choices for the betterment of this team and have to keep their best interests my focus. Wiley said it right when he told the guys he doesn't see individuals—only a solid unit. I knew the solid unit was not properly working, so I jumped on the chance to fix it.

My thoughts flip back to Wiley and his last game. I've watched the video of not only his injury, but the entire game up to that horrible accident more times than I care to admit. Those three linemen were clearly intoxicated. Reports later confirmed it and they were delivered temporary suspensions, while Wiley was forced into a permanent one. Would the accident still have occurred regardless? Who's to say? But when both those defensive linebackers broke through like butter with one taking Wiley in one direction while the other took his leg in another, the football nation dropped to their knees to mourn.

I can't have that on my clock if it's preventable, so Jones had to go.

*****

"A trade offer came in late Monday night from Florida. We felt it was in the best interest of the team to act upon it. Keller was offered in exchange for Jones," Cooper says from the head of the long table.

The rustling of papers is the only sound in the conference room as staff and coaches look over the trade agreement.

"Keller is five seconds slower at the line than Jones." The offensive coach grouches this out with other coaches murmuring in agreement. To say the tension in the room is thick would be an understatement.

"He may not be as talented as Jones, but Keller is dedicated. And more importantly, he's eager to improve. You can work with that." Cooper steeples his fingers and allows the coaches to voice several more questions and concerns before answering each inquiry with patience.

I sit quietly, feeling like I've already done enough, and let Dad take the lead in the meeting. Another paper is handed out and I know all about it, too. Wiley didn't and it's evident when he releases a harsh sigh from across the table. He's sitting right in front of me, but is being diligent on not acknowledging me.

"There was no way we could have predicted such an outcome, but I'm thankful Miss Shaw went with her instincts on this. Jones got off the plane Wednesday morning and was deep in celebrating his trade that night. This morning Miss Shaw received this email." Cooper leans forward and taps the paper. "A sixteen-year-old girl claims he sexually assaulted her at the party, and charges are being brought up against him. I hate this has happened to the girl, but am relieved we didn't let him soil our team with his stupidity. For that, thank you, Miss Shaw, for making the hasty decision. I know you didn't make it lightly."

I nod my head at Dad, knowing he's trying to alleviate my guilt for not including Wiley.

"Black, is there anything you would like to add?" Dad asks him but I keep my eyes on the paper in front of me instead of glancing across the table.

"No, sir, Mr. Cooper. I think you covered it all." Wiley's voice is tight but respectable.

"Then I guess we're done here." Dad dismisses everyone, but I stay in my chair. I'm the one who requested him to stay back this time.

A silent pause flints through the room, before he asks, "What is it, Samantha?"

I roll a pen back and forth, focusing on it with blurry eyes. "I knew better than to break my own rules and look at the mess it's caused."

I've been stubbornly jutting my chin out all morning, hoping to keep an unyielding façade in place. But it slips down now with a few tears following suit. And this isn't me. I don't act like a baby on matters. Again, a consequence for breaking my rules.

Dad moves from his spot and takes up the seat beside me. "Sam… Don't let business get in the way of what you have with Black."

"That was a mistake."

"We blindsided him. He has a right to be angry. He'll settle down and get over it. Don't give up on something with so much potential."

"No. It's best to walk away from it now. Nothing much to lose." I wipe the tears away and try bucking up. "As for the rest of this season, I want no one allowed on the field until six-thirty. That'll give me time to do my job. I'll be in the box suite with you for the remaining three home games, but don't request me to be at the team celebrations or other functions where the coaches and players are included until after the season wraps."

"Samantha—"

"It's business. And that's all there is to it." I collect my papers and hurry out the door. My chin musters enough bravado to jut back out long enough for me to make it to my office.

Chapter Ten

The great gift about living in southern Texas is that the winter pretty much leaves us the heck alone. It's been a mild December. Unfortunately, the gulf has been kicking up some ornery storms and shoving them in our direction. Today is no different. Sitting in my office, I glare at the torrential downpour just outside my window. The stadium is flooded.

My phone pings a message from the travel agent, confirming the flight plans for Wiley's parents and two younger brothers. I'm flying them out here to spend Christmas with him. Maggie promised to not let him know this is my gift to him. All of his family lives a long ways away in Kentucky, so I think it would do him good to have their unexpected company during this holiday. I want him happy here, and at the moment, I know he's not.

A knock sounds at my door, producing Trey.

"What's up?" I ask absently as I set the phone down.

"Black has the team on the field."

"Why on earth is he doing that?"

"Says he wants them conditioned for a rainy game. Looks like that's what they will be playing this week. Pretty smart, beings that nice and dry Arizona won't be prepared for it."

"Tell him to hit the practice field then." I shoo him away.

Ten minutes later, Trey is back at my door and is sopping wet. "He's not budging."

I point him back out the door. "Go tell him again. Don't let him push you around."

My pep talk obviously gives Trey no encouragement—with a deep frown and drooping *dripping* shoulders, he heads back out.

This time he's back in only five minutes. "Black says no," he says at the door and scurries away before I can order him for the third time.

Shoving away from the desk, I shrug on my raincoat and prepare to go to battle. One thing I've learned the hard way is that Wiley Black doesn't get over something very easily. I know this is him trying to regain his muscle over me. Well, I'll show him.

I storm onto the field and right up to Coach Jerk. "You have five minutes to get off my field," I shout over the roar of the loud rain.

"No. This is what they will be playing in this weekend. They need to be prepared." His arms are crossed and his attention stays firmly on the play the guys are performing.

"Then go to the practice field. It's got to be in better shape than this one. You've ruined it!" I'm livid as I focus on the gnarly mud puddles these brutes have made on my poor field.

"Get off my field." His anger rings out over the echoing downpour.

"Your field? Your field? The papers on this place declare this field belonging to me. Now *you* get off!" I've just noticed the players have paused and are taking in this standoff.

"No—"

"Don't tell me no. You're mad. I get it, but it's time for you to get over it." I shove him slightly, but the action was fruitless with him not budging a single centimeter. "Off. Now!"

Wiley still stands here leering at me. If he wants to be a jerk, then I can up him on that factor right back. I turn on my muddy heels to go call security to have him removed. I don't even get a foot away before I find myself being reeled back around. I meet none other than Wiley's fervent lips.

Stunned.

I'm stunned, because I didn't see that one coming at all. The kiss is aggressive and filled with rage and I'm too shocked to choose between liking it or not.

Catcalls and whistles snap me out of the shock, and so I decide I most definitely don't like it. Before I can register what I've done, my hand lashes out and smacks the side of his face. I hold my stinging hand and watch as a red handprint blossoms across his left cheek. And I swear to you, steam is rising from this fuming giant. My heart skips several beats and then takes off in a sprint.

Without releasing me from the snare of his glower, Wiley points to the tunnel. "Practice is over. Go home!" He yells to his team and the soggy players run like their wet butts are on fire—knowing it's in their best interest. Smart men. I want to run, too, but I'm frozen in place.

In the heat of things, both our raincoat hoods have fallen down and we both stand here now with hair plastered from the downpour. Droplets trickle down my neck and onto my back, but I don't mind. The embarrassment has seared my face so the cool wetness is welcomed. If I could disappear on the spot, I would. But since that's not going to happen, so I stand my squishy ground and wait for the field to be cleared.

Once we're alone, I lay into him. "You ever disrespect me like that again in front my team, I'll have you kicked out on your behind. And if you so much as set a foot on this field during a drizzle for anything other than game day, you'll be slapped with a fine so fast your head will spin." I take a step back and stab a finger in his direction. "You have a practice field. Use it."

Wiley grabs my arm before I can flee. "That... That was unprofessional. I... You drive me crazy. I'm mad at you, but—"

"I'm not on a power trip and don't need you constantly putting me in my place. You're mad. I'm sorry, but business is business." With a defeated shake of my head, I wiggle out of his grasp and motion between us. "This was a mistake. I won't allow it to affect this team."

I give Wiley a few seconds to respond. When he doesn't, I start dredging through the mud and toward the tunnel, feeling the weight of the rain and this decision all the way down to my bones. It's too much of a burden, but what's done is done.

*****

Sitting on the damp concrete floor, my focus is on the verse written along the wall. I read it aloud, hoping the words will reveal something new to me.

"Therefore, since we are surrounded by such a great cloud of witnesses, let us throw off everything that hinders and the sin that so easily entangles, and let us run with perseverance the race marked out for us." I say it once more silently as the somber melody of the rain keeps me company.

The print is in black and gold boldness and easily grabs your attention. I wonder if all of this time I've missed the significance within this verse. I've spent the past several years on a distinct course, but now it seems maybe I've not run the right race. For the race I've picked has been a lonely one.

As I'm pondering this, the bold clattering of dress shoes sound throughout the tunnel. Cooper appears from around the bend and joins me on the floor. What a contrast of genes—daughter in work uniform and father in high-dollar business suit.

"You smacked him good." He says this on a chuckle as he nudges my shoulder with his own.

"He deserved it."

"Absolutely."

"Are you watching too many security episodes again?"

"No. I saw his face in person."

"You did?"

Dad nods his head. "He came by to apologize and ask that I not castrate him. I made him no promises."

"Don't castrate him, Dad. It's just as much my fault as his." I release a long sigh. "I just don't know what to do."

"We've only got a handful of games left. How about we get through the season without the two of you declaring war. Okay?"

"Yes, sir."

I rest my head on Dad's shoulder and just be his daughter for a spell. The familiar scent of Polo reminds me of Sunday mornings when I was much younger. My favorite spot during worship service was the crook of Dad's arm and by the time the preacher said amen, I'd somehow picked up his cologne and carried it the remainder of the day. It's a nostalgic smell of comfort and much needed at the moment.

We simply sit and listen to the rhythmic pinging of the rain. Thank goodness, the rhythm is finally letting up, even if the hurt in my chest isn't.

"Are you happy?" Dad asks after a while.

I wasn't expecting that. I shrug my shoulder, not knowing the answer. "Sure. I guess."

"Samantha." His voice requests a more truthful answer.

"I'm just... I'm lonely."

"You don't have to be lonely. That's a choice you can control."

"I'm not moving back in with you and Mom," I say adamantly, causing him to chuckle.

"You know what I mean, young lady."

"Yes, sir."

Dad slowly makes his way back to standing and moves over to the verse. Tapping his fingers to the word *hinder*, he says, "Don't let fear hinder you from the blessing God has prepared for you." Dad tips his head in my direction and begins walking away. Before he gets too far down the tunnel, he says over his shoulder, "Any given moment."

I say nothing in return, because I'm pretty sure I've failed in this moment.

Chapter Eleven

The season comes to a close with a finish of 10 to 6, with one playoff win. All in all, not a bad conclusion. It's not stellar, but there's lots of potential for next year. I think we are pretty set with a sturdy team, so there won't be much work to do during the draft this year.

The holidays came and went with Wiley keeping his distance. I did receive a lovely card from Maggie, thanking me and letting me know they had a wonderful Christmas in Texas. I've decided Wiley keeping his distance has been a good thing—most days, anyway—because when we are around each other it's beyond awkward. He's taken up sitting on the other side of the church with a row full of his players. I guess that's for the best, because this odd ache has formed in my chest and worsens when he's around.

I don't get it. How can a few kisses and only a handful of stolen moments together merit such grievance? The past seven months flicker through my mind and all I can see is Wiley Black. There have only been a limited amount of days in there where his presence was absent. Admittedly, I got attached to him without realizing it.

With great effort, I tamp the ache down as best as I can and focus on the job before me tonight. Smoothing my glittery frock with nervous hands, I listen as another reporter asks the same question I've already answered a few times since arriving at the postseason celebration.

"Tell me, Miss Shaw. What's your take on this young team of yours?"

"You've watched them this season, Henry. We both know they played a respectable game. They can only go up from here, and it's going to be one impressive climb."

"Will they win the play-offs next year?" Henry asks as if he fully believes I can magically see into the future.

"I have no doubt. Wiley Black is one talented coach and he will see to it." My words are full of certainty. Taking my focus off Henry, I scan the stadium's decked-out lobby. It's massive and perfect for such a grand party as tonight. Just off to the right, I catch sight of Wiley. It's obvious he's listened to the exchange with me and the reporter. I excuse myself to go congratulate him.

Wiley's usual reserved demeanor must be taking the night off, and in its place something close to an amused smirk twitches at his lips. Those wicked green eyes meet mine just briefly before giving my frilly dress—that I had no choice in—a full inspection.

"You look like a—"

"Don't—"

"Fairy Princess." He leans over my shoulder and seems to be searching for something on my back.

"What are you doing?" I crane my neck to see what's got his attention.

"Looking for your wings."

His nice, lean torso is right in front of me—making it easy to deliver a playful punch.

"You're not funny," I mutter before stealing a whiff of his subtle cologne. He's so close and my hands tingle to reach out and close the tiny distance between us—to run my fingers along the inviting scruff on his cheek.

He seems to be on the same page, because he makes no move to back off. "Seriously, you look beautiful."

"Thank you. You don't look too shabby yourself." My eyes roam the tailored dark-gray suit that fits him impeccably. The ache in my chest squeezes tighter as he dances his fingertips along my neck and on towards my bare shoulder and arm.

Leaning close to my ear, he whispers, "You know that saying is true."

I have to forcefully swallow my emotions to ask, "What saying?"

"You don't know what you've got until it's gone."

A trance overtakes us as the tension pushes at my lonely soul. This man fills so many voids. Voids I didn't know I had until he showed up. The intimate bubble is short-lived as some other reporter calls Wiley's attention. Wiley eases back slightly to give me one last look before turning to answer the guy, who I want to physically hurt for interrupting us.

Leaving him to it, I mingle back through the crowd for the next longest. Photo ops with Mom and Dad, a few quick quotes to the press, and congratulating the teammates and coaches keep me busy and I end up losing sight of Wiley. Disappointedly, I head out into the chilly night and focus on the spring ahead. There is a lot to do with three concerts and two rodeos on the books.

Making mental notes, I open my door and climb in the cab. I'm struck by fear immediately at finding someone waiting on the passenger side. Releasing a scream riddled in terror, I let my fists fly in self-defense.

"Knock it off before you hurt yourself." Wiley gathers my wrists in one hand, putting an abrupt stop to my feeble attempt at protecting myself.

"Are you trying to end me with a heart attack?" I wrench one hand free to comfort the pounding in my chest. Wiley refuses to give me back my right hand and somehow that helps soothe the ache a little.

Sniffing back unwelcomed tears, I ask, "What are you doing, Wiley?"

"Dang it, Sam. I really miss your stubborn behind."

"We both have jobs to do, and we've seen how *we*

can bite us in the butt. I'm talking scars." Truthfully, it was inflicted on my heart—not my butt.

"I think it would be worth the scars," he says adamantly.

I have nothing to say to that, which is good because Wiley doesn't give me the opportunity. Reaching over and entwining his fingers through my hair, he grazes his lips tenderly over my own. What a contradiction Hermes can be—one minute he's Mr. Rough and Tough and then the next he's the sweetest, gentlest creature I've ever been blessed to know.

Those warm lips dance a confession with mine until I'm dizzy and those traitorous tears spill freely.

Wiping them away with his thumbs, he whispers, "I'm in love with you. You'd be worth any scar, Samantha Shaw."

His words cause my heart to swell and rob me of my voice. All I can do is sit frozen and watch him climb out of the truck. I keep my eyes focused on him until he disappears into the dark parking lot.

I'm so stubborn with everything, especially my emotions. I normally keep them so bottled up that if something or someone ever triggers them, I erupt into a hot mess. Sitting in my rusty antique truck in my gold, glittery dress, I blubber like a baby.

Chapter Twelve

The aroma of fried, sweet goodness keeps tickling my nose as I carry the five boxes of Krispy Kreme donuts down the too-long hallway. My mouth waters with knowing the warm treats are going to go down effortlessly.

"I need one now. This is torture," Trey whines as we walk towards the break room with him carrying the other five boxes.

"Me too, but hold your horses. We've got business to take care of first." I push the door open with my backside and greet a bunch of hungry workers. Placing the boxes down, I have to automatically pop Buck's hand away from sneaking in the top box. "Wait a minute, old man."

He grumbles something while Benji hands over the bowl with each crew member's name scribbled on a separate slip of paper.

"All right, this year's season-ending cleanup is upon us again. Our department got divvied out the chore of cleaning the stadium seats in sections E and F. Same rules as last year. Three names get drawn from the bowl. Those three have to race to eat a dozen donuts the fastest. Loser gets the job."

I nod at Benji to begin. He pulls the first slip and grins. "Sam." Everybody else grumbles.

I'm the queen of the donut-eating contests around here. All's good for me. I get to pig out on donuts and don't have to worry about scraping gum and other mess off the seats.

Benji pulls another name. "Colton." Colton rolls his eyes and we laugh. He has a weird gag reflex and can't eat fast. Too bad! "Last name is John." John is the new guy, so I have no idea what I'm up against. He's scrawny like me, but I know all too well that those are the ones you have to worry about.

Someone clears his throat by the door. Looking over, I find Wiley watching on curiously.

"I smell donuts," he says.

"You can't have one. These are business donuts. You—"

Before I can continue, Buck interrupts. "We're just having a fun donut-eating contest. You're more than welcome to participate." Mischief dances in his dark eyes.

Wiley crosses arms. "Yeah? What's at stake?"

"Loser has to clean the stadium seats. Poor Sam's name got drawn. There's no way that puny girl is beating Colton. The guy is a donut-eating machine."

I notice Buck is making it sound like a two person challenge. I also notice everyone playing along and not correcting him. No one wants the seat-cleaning duty. Buck hands me a box and is about to hand Colton his, but pauses to cut Wiley a look. I turn away and take my place at the table so he doesn't catch my grin.

"I bet a big guy like you could polish off a dozen with no problem."

I look over and see Wiley's big ego broadcasting as he smirks at me. "I just have to eat a dozen faster than her and she has to clean the seats?"

Buck and the other guys murmur all kinds of encouragement, but Zane looks confused.

"Sam always wi—" Zane starts but Colton grabs a donut and shoves it in his mouth before Zane finishes.

Wiley's back is turned, so he doesn't catch on to the ruckus. He's too busy sidling up beside me, looking way too smug for his own good.

"If we only have to eat a dozen, why do you have so many boxes?" He motions to the tall stack at the end of the table.

"Hello. The *hot* sign was on." Trey exaggerates his words while shaking his head.

I nudge Wiley's side. "Don't you have coach duties to worry about?"

"It won't take long to beat you. Say, you want to sweeten the deal?" The green twinkles in his eyes. He so thinks he's got this in the bag.

"Why on earth would I do that if you're favored to win this?" I pout for good measure. Turning my attention away from him, I pop open my lid and start stacking the donuts—six in each stack. The scent is heavenly and I can't stop licking my lips.

"What are you doing?" Wiley asks as he opens the lid to his box.

I shrug my shoulder. "I thought maybe it would be quicker to grab one, if they are in stacks." I try to sound naïve—like I'm figuring this out on the fly.

My crew snorts and snickers, adding to me sounding like an idiot.

"Come on, Sam. Let's add to the challenge. Be a good losing sport for a change," Colton antagonizes. He looks relieved now that he's not my opponent.

"Look what you've gotten me into, Coach," I mutter, trying to seem like I only want him to hear.

"How about the loser has to wear a pair of hot-pink rubber gloves and a tutu while cleaning!" Benji barks this out during a fit of laughter.

"And one of those sparkly tiaras," Trey adds. The crowd rings out in laughter.

Wiley joins in, adding his own chuckle. Oh, he's so sure of himself. "Come on, Peaches. I'd love to see you in a tutu."

I pop my sticky hand on my hip. "Who's to say I'm gonna lose?" I have to show some confidence for good measure. He somehow knows me too well and will catch on if I'm not careful.

He pats me on the shoulder. "Then you should have no trouble agreeing to the bet."

I scan the eager crowd, surrounding us at the table—cellphones poised to catch the contest on video.

Releasing a frustrated sigh, I say, "Sure. I'll take one for the team. That's the kind of teammate I am."

"Good. Good. Let's get this going. On the count of three, you two eat up." Buck instructs us as Wiley turns his hat on backwards as if it may slow him down otherwise. I try not to notice how blame cute he looks.

When Buck gets to three, Wiley snatches up his first and it's gone in two bites. I simultaneously slam my hands down forcefully on top of the stacks and smash them to form two manageable donut sandwiches. One sandwich takes three bites, the second one take five bites, and I'm done. Wiley is on his eighth donut and doesn't seem to grasp the fact that my box is already empty. The break room erupts in laughter and shouts.

"Y'all just played me," Wiley mumbles around a mouthful of donut. He plops in a seat and just keeps eating for the heck of it.

"You lost, dude. You don't have to keep eating," Zane says.

"You jerks think you're so funny. I'm finishing my donuts." Wiley stands up and swipes every box, but one. "As a matter of fact, I think I've earned all of these for that dirty trick." He storms out the door, with the crowd grumbling in good humor while diving for the abandoned box.

*****

"You totally rock a pink tutu, Coach." I snicker as I plop down in the stadium seat a row up from him.

He ignores me as he works on scraping a stubborn piece of gum off the bottom of the seat he's working on.

"And that tiara looks so sweet in the midst of all that dark hair." My tone is full of mockery.

He finally gets the gum free and tosses it in the garbage bag beside him. I wonder where on earth Buck found a pair of hot-pink rubber gloves big enough for Wiley. Undoubtedly, a cleaning supply store exists for giants.

"You want to grab a donut when you're finished?" I ask. This earns me only a sharp glare. "Our little race has already gone viral. We should celebrate." I've watched it a half dozen times myself. The dumbfounded look on Wiley's face when he realized I won is priceless.

"I don't like you." He grumbles this out before scooting down to the next seat. I shuffle one down, too, to keep him company. The place is deserted with the team on hiatus.

"But you said you loved me the other night." I say this to joke around, but when he looks up, I notice there's nothing funny about the statement.

"And I meant it." Sharp conviction laces his tone.

"But you hardly know me."

He huffs out a faint cloud of aggravation—it's actually cold enough today to see your breath.

115

Peeling the silly gloves, tiara, and tutu off, Wiley climbs over the row and takes the seat beside me. My body betrays me and shivers with him being near. Mistaking this as a sign of me being cold, Wiley reaches over and buttons the two wayward buttons on my coat before wrapping his arm around me. This gesture is so thoughtfully tender, and I gladly melt into his warmth.

"You know I know you. I've known you since the day we met."

Glancing up from where I'm resting on his shoulder, I scoff. "That sounded convoluted."

"You're gonna tell me you didn't feel the connection that first day?" He gives me a challenging look—an eyebrow raised and lips pursed.

"Yes, but there's just too much at risk here."

"The only thing I see at risk is us losing out on something extraordinary over our stupid stubbornness."

I'm about to rebuke, but Wiley's lips brush against my own, causing me to forget my name. It's just a simple closed-mouth kiss, but it really makes a statement. It's slow and lingering.

Pressing his forehead to mine, Wiley whispers, "I thank God for allowing my injury."

I try to pull away, but he cups both his hands to my face to keep me. "How can you say that?"

"That injury led me down a path straight to you. You're the biggest blessing I've ever stumbled upon, and I thank Him for not letting me miss out on it.

Without the injury, I would have." Another kiss renders me close to tears.

Eventually I pull back and ask, "What about our fallout?"

"Not a fallout, Peaches. Just a bump in our hard-headed road. How about giving us another chance?"

I ponder the idea of tangling with him again. The idea is terrifyingly tempting. I sure do miss him. "I suppose we could try being friends…"

His low, raspy chuckle sends a shiver along my stunned body. "Baby, you can call this…" He motions between us. "Friends, buddies, whatever, but let's be clear on the fact that you're mine."

His lips meet mine again, but this time there's nothing slow and sweet about it. It's a demanding claim that says all I need to know. He's mine, too.

"I love you," I say against his lips, not wanting to lose the connection.

"I know." There's no smugness in his declaration—only a reverent awe.

Chapter Thirteen

They say spring is a time for renewal, a fresh start. I'm beginning to think someone might just be right. Everyone has kept busy. The team is on break, so Wiley has been back to Kentucky for the last two weeks but we text or talk most days.

Wiley and I have managed to find an acceptable groove for our relationship—whatever that is. We bicker one minute and make out the next when we are around each other. I have no idea what I'm doing, but I sure am having fun trying to figure it out. We'll have to see how this groove holds up next season, though.

We've worked in a few more drag races with me letting him beat me once. The man has an ego that is too needy, so a girl's gotta do what a girl's gotta do. He did gift me with his own victory dance. And just let me say for the record—those nice, lean hips know how to shimmy. I've been tempted to let him win a few more times just for the show, but I'm too competitive for that.

We hang out at the ranch a good bit as well—

fishing in the lake and horseback riding around the property. It's a nice change to see him away from the stadium and football world.

The Bobcats are a few months away from training camp, so they are on a mandatory vacation from the field, but are due back next week to start weight training and meetings. I've had the field to myself and it's been heavenly. I've treated the vibrant turf to lots of nourishment and aerations and such for the last few weeks. It'll be raring to go soon.

A familiar knock sounds on my door, producing a reluctant Trey.

"What now?"

He scratches through his dark-blond hair, trying to figure out what to say. It's a Trey tell I've picked up over the years when he's nervous.

"Just spit it out." I narrow my eyes at him.

Sighing, he says, "Black and the team are back early."

"Okay."

"They're on the field."

Talk about déjà vu. Ugh. "Tell them to get off or else." I point for him to get on with it, but Trey just throws his hands up in defeat.

"I already did. He's refusing just like last time. You handle it." He has enough nerve to give me a stern glare before dashing off.

Mumbling a few sentiments under my breath, I stomp down to the field and find the players dressed for weight training. There's some comfort in not finding them dressed in cleats and shoulder pads.

Sidling right up to Wiley, I try to hide my giddiness over seeing him and say firmly, "No player is allowed on this field for at least two more months and you know it." Crossing my arms, I wait for another one of his bull-headed showdowns.

"They're not technically on the field." He points over to where the team is standing on the sideline. "I'm trying to explain a new play I've been working on, but they're not getting it. I need to show them. You have perfect timing. You can help me out."

I shake my head vigorously in disapproval. "Nah-uh. Last time I played with you, I couldn't grip my coffee cup for a week. No thanks." I hear a chuckle skirt along the players, but ignore it.

"No. Nothing like that. I'll behave this time." Wiley tilts his head and winks at me.

Confused, but not wanting to disrespect him in front of his team again—and let's be honest, between the Jones trade and the slap I've done my share—I reluctantly agree.

"Leave your hat and shades on the sideline. They'll get in the way," Wiley says over his shoulder as he grabs a ball and heads to the fifty.

I yank both off and toss them to the ground before following him. Placing me before him, he sets the ball on his side of the line of scrimmage.

"I'm offense, right?"

His smug look is all the answer I need, but he says anyway, "No. I am."

"I hate playing defense." That sounded sort of whiny even to my ears.

"Suck it up this once." He points at me to stay put as he turns to address his team.

That's perfectly fine by me, because I'm left with a fine view of his nicely round backside. I'm a huge fan of his rigorous squat routines. Those track pants sure know how to show off all his effort.

"All right, what have I told you is the most important part of this sport of football?" He barks out full of commanding attitude that demands respect. I already have goose bumps.

"Teamwork!" The team's voices ring out.

"And who should always have your back?"

"Your Teammates!"

"You've got to have one another's backs. No matter the outcome." Pointing to the line where the football is resting beside it, he says, "You need a teammate that's going to go to this line of scrimmage prepared to go to battle *with* you."

He paces a few steps, looks over his shoulder at me briefly, and continues to address his guys. "A new season is nearing and we need to be clear on a few things. You need a teammate who's always looking out for your safety and is willing to put you in your place if need be. If you can't depend on your team, then you have nothing in this game."

The guys nod their heads, acknowledging they get it. He must feel confident they do, because he turns back and meets me at the line of scrimmage.

"You ready, Peaches?"

Please don't hurt me!

I brace myself and bravely say, "Lay it on me, Coach." I just know he's going to knock me on my rear to even the score between us. Maybe I deserve it. Either way, I'm gonna take it like the tough Texan I am.

Wiley Black's large form kneels in front of me and the football. Then he shows me the play, and I'm so lightheaded from the rush of it I see stars. Blinking them away as best I can, I focus on the diamond ring pinched between his fingers.

"You say you go with your gut on decisions that matter the most. That true?" The harsh alpha male façade has vanished leaving behind that gentle giant I've grown so attached to.

"You know it's true." Tears push their way free.

"Well, I've come to one of those decisions. I want you… No. I *need* you in my life."

"You know we clash professionally. What about the effect this will have on the team?" I try to hold on tight to my rational side, but it's slipping fast.

"Baby, I only see us going up from here and I guarantee the climb will be impressive." He steals my quote, but I don't mind. It sounds really nice coming from him. Pulling my left hand in his, Wiley asks, "Will you marry this washed-up football player?"

"No." I bat the tears away with my free hand.

"No?" A confused hurt furrows his brows as he glances at his team nervously.

Pulling his face back towards me, I say, "No, but I will agree to marry this incredible man who is a great football player and an even better coach."

A lopsided grin pulls at those handsome lips. "So, is that a yes?"

"Yes, Coach. I'll marry you."

Slipping the ring on my finger, Wiley claims my lips. Whistles and catcalls ring out from his team, but this time I don't mind. The kiss is triumphant and hard to maintain with us both grinning.

"Team, you're dismissed," Wiley orders and goes right back to kissing me on the fifty yard line.

I pull away to catch my breath and giggle like a lovesick girl. "Dad's going to be glued to the security tapes tonight."

"Nah. He just saw it live with your mom, my parents, and your crew right along with our team." It didn't get past me, he just said *our* team. I really like the sound of that.

I squint up at Wiley. He looks so proud of himself. "What?"

He turns towards the box suite windows and gives the hidden audience a thumbs-up. And that's when I see them all—hands in the air clapping. This man made sure everyone important to us witnessed his proposal and that just turns me into a swooning mess.

Turning back to me, giving them no more regard, Wiley beckons me to lay on the fifty yard line with him.

The sun is shining gloriously today and is most fitting with how I feel. Side by side, holding hands, I ask, "So, what are we celebrating?"

Before answering, Wiley leans over and presses another kiss to my willing lips. "The best reverse play I ever called."

"Well played, Coach." I can't help but grin. He most certainly called it right. I'm so glad he was brave enough to push us in another direction and didn't allow me to throw the towel in a few months back when things got too tough.

"Any given moment," Wiley whispers.

"Any given moment," I whisper back.

2 Seasons Later...

I'm close to marching on that blame field and slapping some sense into my husband. The man has me all worked up tonight.

"Come on, Black!" I yell from the box suite as though he could hear me. The defense looks like they're napping, for crying out loud. My eyes scan this pristine stadium in appreciation, even though it's not mine, as I try to calm down.

Wiley's biggest cheerleader, aka Maggie, pats my shoulder. "You should calm down, dear. My Wiley will get the job done."

My eyes focus back on that handsome devil standing on the sideline as he shouts into his headset. Yanking them off moments later, he commences to yelling at his defensive coach. There's tension prickling the air in anticipation. So close...

"Maggie, the defense can't sleep just yet. We've got to hold 'em. We were right here last year. The game of all games and we lost it in overtime. Tonight, I don't have *time* for overtime!"

As though Wiley can sense me sassing, he

abruptly turns in my direction and points sternly. Maggie and Mom giggle. There's absolutely no way he can see me!

"It's not funny." I feel the sweat accumulating on my forehead from being so worked up. I swipe it off with the palm of my hand as I huff. "That man is always thinking he can boss me around."

"Someone needs to," Cooper says on a chuckle.

I shoot him a glare before focusing back on the game. The guys are scrambling around to line up for the next play. "How much time is left on the clock?" I ask no one in particular.

"Three minutes, fifteen seconds," Nolan answers.

My nervous hand runs over my aching gut. "Hold 'em, defense." I yell and luckily they listen.

A few more unproductive plays from the opposing team pass with the Bobcats finally regaining control of the ball. Wiley uses their last timeout, so I sit back and take a few deep breaths to steady my nerves.

"Are you okay, darlin'?" Mom asks as she rubs my arm. Everyone is coddling me tonight, and it's raking my nerves just as bad as this game.

"Sure, sure." I brush her off as I watch on.

Next thing I know, some teenage kid is tapping me on the shoulder. I turn to eye the pimply guy with irritation. He's an assistant on the sidelines—hands out water and towels.

"Yes?"

"Mrs. Black, Coach said to tell you to chill out.

Says you best not work yourself up into going into labor during the most important game of his career."

I growl and the boy cautiously takes a step back. "You tell Coach to mind his business on the field and not to be worrying about me. Tell him to get the job done." I release the words through gritted teeth.

The kid flees from the room. He's smarter than I thought.

Turning my focus back to the field, I watch as the offense positions themselves at the line of scrimmage. An ache flickers across my back and races around to my bellybutton. I try to discreetly breathe through the pain, but Mom catches me this time.

"Samantha Black! You really are in labor!"

Yep. Contractions began right before halftime. I smirk through the pain, thinking that my husband—way out there on that field figured it out before this crowd surrounding me. *How'd he do that anyway?*

"I'm fine. It's okay." I huff the words out as the contraction fizzles out.

Everyone is swarming around me like I've just fallen apart and they are scurrying to figure out how to fix me. Maggie is grinning ear to ear, while trying to coerce a cup of water in my hand. Rolling my eyes and brushing off their concerns, I watch in awe as Grant throws a perfect spiral downfield, landing right into the wide receivers waiting hands. Timmons catches it beautifully at the twenty, before being tackled.

Time is rapidly ticking down. It's now or never.

The offense lines up quickly with Grant stealing glances at the timeclock.

"Come on, Grant!" I yell. "Get it done!" He has to get it done. There's little time left with the ballgame tied. I seriously don't need an overtime. I really don't know how much more time this impatient kid is going to stay put. I grip my round belly and silently beg my baby for another hour or so.

I hear Cooper on the phone, but keep my gaze on the field. "I need a car ready to take Mrs. Black to the hospital. ASAP."

I'm not worried. Wiley and I met with the OB/GYN last month to form a labor plan here in California. My other doctor advised it; once it was pretty evident the Bobcats would be here.

Wiley has also been giving my abdomen several pep talks in the last few weeks. Just last night, he delivered one final talk. With his hat turned backwards, still wearing his coach's attire of T-shirt and track pants, Wiley knelt before me and began running his hands along my rounded belly.

"Son, we've all got a job to do. Mine is to lead the Bobcats to victory. Yours is to stay put until I do so." He placed a kiss near my bellybutton before he continued. "And you could also stop giving your mom heartburn. I'm tired of hearing her whine about it." Wiley told our son all of this in his coach's voice, looking adorable. Those green eyes sparkled proudly.

That snide heartburn comment earned Wiley a playful smack upside the head. I kissed him confused afterwards, so all's good. I lick my lips just thinking about that man's sweet kisses. They've only gotten sweeter. I do believe God created Wiley Black just for me. Nothing has ever fit so right in all my life.

Another contraction clamps down just as Grant performs a perfect quarterback sneak, scoring a touchdown. We all erupt in cheers. With only mere seconds left on the timeclock, it's a done deal. The field is swarmed and confetti flurries out in celebration.

I'm jumping up and down in victory when I feel it—an odd tug and then warmth. Yep. My water just broke. The little guy held off like a good son for his daddy. Nodding towards Cooper, he takes my arm and leads me to the awaiting car. Mom is left to go help Maggie and Nolan round up their son.

*****

Wiley Nolan Black Jr. was born exactly forty-eight minutes after his daddy led his team to win the game of a lifetime. And that, my friends, is one epic season of life!

"To every *thing there is* a season, and a time to every purpose under the heaven." Ecclesiastes 3:1.

Any Given Moment Playlist

"Quarterback" by Kopecky
"Centuries" by Fall Out Boy
"Flashed Junk Mind" by Milky Chance
"Bright" by Echosmith
"Peaches" by In The Valley Below
"Cornerstone" by Hillsong Live
"Lay 'Em Down" by Need to Breathe
"Hey There Delilah" by Plain White T's
"Awake and Alive" by Skillet

ABOUT THE AUTHOR

Bestselling author T.I. Lowe sees herself as an ordinary country girl who loves to tell extraordinary stories. She knows she's just getting started and has many more stories to tell. A wife and mother and active in her church community, she resides in coastal South Carolina with her family.

For a complete list of Lowe's published books, biography, upcoming events, and other information, visit tilowe.com and be sure to check out her blog, COFFEE CUP, while you're there!

She would love to hear from you!!
ti.lowe@yahoo.com
twitter: TiLowe
facebook: T.I. Lowe

Made in the USA
Coppell, TX
28 October 2022